DEBBIE WEBB & MARY OWEN

↓↑⌒↑↓™

WITNESS

VERBATIM
P R E S S

Published by Verbatim Press

WITNESS

DEDICATION

This work is lovingly dedicated to Alton Howard...
...loving father, faithful friend,
and humble servant of the Almighty.

NOTE TO READER

This book is neither a novel nor a biographical sketch, but a fictitious narrative intended as a testimony to the life and conversion of an actual person—Mary Magdalene—one of the itinerant followers of Jesus.

In his book, *the five people you meet in heaven*, Mitch Albom made this striking claim: "No story sits by itself. Sometimes stories meet at corners and sometimes they cover one another completely, like stones beneath a river."[1]

Mary's story, though ancient history, more than meets at the corners of our contemporary lives. It overlaps into the deepest chambers of our hearts and touches us where we most need touching.

While the authors' rendering of the Magdalene's story is imaginative, the true account of Mary's journey is recorded in the Book of Life as an eternal witness to the grace of the Messiah she loved so passionately...

If you wish to read actual scriptural accounts of these events, please refer to:

Chapter One—John 8:2-11
Chapter Two—Luke 7:36-50; Luke 8:1-3
Chapter Three—John 20:1-18
Chapter Four—Mark 15:33-41
Chapter Five—Mark 5:21-43

---

[1] Mitch Albom, *the five people you meet in heaven* (New York: Hyperion 2003)

PROLOGUE

NEAR A SMALL TOWN IN ISRAEL, AN ANCIENT GRAVE
SURRENDERS ITS SECRET...
     FIVE SCROLLS...
     ...MESSAGES ENTOMBED WITH THEIR SCRIBE;
     A CUSTOM OF RESPECT FOR THE DEAD.

A PECULIAR MOTIF MARKS THE BURIAL SITE...
     FIVE SYMBOLS...
     ...INSCRIBED ON THE PARCHMENTS,
     ...ETCHED INTO THE WALL OF THE TOMB,
       ...ENGRAVED ON A PENDANT FOUND
        AMONGST THE GRAVE CLOTHES.

         ONCE TRANSLATED, THE LETTERS
         REVEAL THE SIGNIFICANCE OF
         THE SYMBOLS.

         THE TOMB'S INHABITANT...

         ...MARY THE MAGDALENE

THE FIRST OF THE FIVE SCROLLS... PENNED IN
THE EARLY SUMMER OF THE YEAR A.D. 35...

MY DEAR PHILIP,

Are you safe?

We were separated so abruptly by the Roman officials. I've made many attempts to reach you. All in vain. I am anxious. I don't know what else to do. I pray night and day for your deliverance.

Remember the pendant? That's what caught the soldier's eye the night we were arrested. You saw him jerk it from my neck, leaving a stinging welt which throbbed through the night.

He dangled it in front of me, mocking me.

Look what I found!

I strained against the ropes binding my wrists, demanding that he give it back; it was a gift.

The arrogant young man held it over his head, teasing me. Then he pushed me back, causing me to stumble.

I fell to my knees.

Cramming the pendant into his pouch, he smirked and taunted me.

This will bring me a handsome reward. After all, it has caused a great deal of controversy among people in high places.

You have no idea how great the controversy really is. Otherwise, you wouldn't be so bold as to scoff.

Is that so?

He clamped his hand around my jaw like a vise. The pain made me wince. Yanking me closer until I couldn't escape his foul breath, he pressed me.

Who do you think you are, assuming to know matters which concern ranking officials?

I took a risk in my hesitant reply.

There are authorities more powerful, greater than even you know.

He laughed, tucking the pouch inside his leather girdle.

What's the point of arguing with him? I scolded myself. He really doesn't know.

It was terrifying, Philip, and ever since that night, I've felt a nagging sense of urgency to write to you… as if time is running out. I find myself pleading with the Lord to keep you safe until I reach you…

Before it is too late…

Before the government halts the spread of letters circulating among us…

Before the grave lays claim to you…

Before Messiah returns.

If any of these things should occur prior to your discovering the truth about Jesus, my heart would be scarred with a deep and inconsolable wound on your behalf. And as for you…

I believe there is a battle being waged for your heart, for the hearts of all ordinary men and women like us. And the outcome, Philip, has far greater significance than you realize.

You must keep that in mind as I attempt to explain this peculiar sequence of events.

I suppose I should take you back to the beginning because the message will have more meaning if you hear my story in its proper… maybe improper, at times… setting.

I am an orphan.

My mother, a Jewish prostitute, surrendered me as an infant to her eldest brother. Poverty had driven her to prostitution. Her father, having died when she was a child, left her without a dowry, and her only sibling—the uncle with whom I lived—was himself a pauper. With no hope of courtship, she was destitute and helpless; left to become a beggar, a harlot, or a victim of starvation. Harlotry, as you know, provides a much more dependable income than the charity of indigent people.

Once pregnant, she couldn't support a child, and a baby was an inconvenient interruption anyway, given her occupation.

My father? All I ever knew about him was that he, too, was a Hebrew. No name. No face. No legacy. No embrace.

My mother died before I discovered the truth about her. I have a vivid memory of her funeral, though, because of the scar it left on my heart.

This is how I remember it...

Though five years old, I am unaware that the corpse lying on the cot is my mother. I listen in a detached but inquisitive way as the relatives and neighbors discuss her. It is clear that they despise her for the disgrace she has caused her family.

One elderly woman clucks her tongue as she chides.

Did you hear where they found her?

The rest of the women spontaneously join in the prattle.

Wasn't she lying on the ground outside a dwelling on the northern edge of Cana? They say she must have been there all night.

I'm sure you heard that she was... well, ...exposed.

Does anyone know what happened?

The elderly woman dominates the conversation.

It was rumored that she was sick; that she had been battling the plague of prostitution for several years. What else would one expect from such loose living?

Do you think that's what killed her?

Could be. Or maybe someone's angry wife took matters into her own hands.

As a matter of fact, didn't I hear that she got caught trying to seduce the youngest son of Abijah in Nain?

Keeping the conversation astir with intrigue, they start over—rehearsing the circumstances of her death again and again.

I sense a morbid delight in the way they recite each detail. It seems to grow darker with each retelling.

I can't understand why they have put a dead woman on trial when she can't offer a defense to their accusations. Isn't her reputation tarnished enough?

Curious, I edge closer to the bier to see what the woman looks like. She appears frail and abandoned, and the bruises on her face and neck bring to my mind a frightening image of violence. I feel sadness in how they are treating her. Something tragic speaks to me from the empty look on her pale, swollen face.

Suddenly, my sorrow is replaced with shock. One of the relatives grabs my arm, whirling me around to face her. Jabbing a finger in my face, she spits words at me in disgust.

And you are the unwanted child she forced on her brother!

No one moves to rescue me. I just stand there, blinking rapidly, as my heart races to catch up with the harsh revelation. And though I don't fully understand what she said, there is no mistaking how she said it.

I feel a burning shame about where I come from, who I am. Her words press into the soft clay of my memory, their hardening imprint throbbing in my temples, pinching at my eyeballs until they sting with scalding tears.

I suppose I had never really felt loved, but I had never considered being unwanted... until now.

Anyone could have predicted what would happen to me—but that's assuming anyone cared. I can still recall the onset of a deep despair...

Every day dawns with the same sadness—the heartache of rejection. I try to fight the feeling of emptiness that has taken root and is growing inside, but I can't fend it off.

I feel like I'm sinking—falling into a frightening void. As if an oppressive shadow is stalking me—settling over me with increasing darkness. It suffocates me with a stifling gloom, bearing down on me until I can hardly hold up under the strain. Finally, it swallows me up, plunging my heart into a thick darkness—so dense that I am drowning in it. A darkness that prevails even in the light of day, isolating me from any hope of human consolation.

There is no one with whom I can share my heartache; no one to whom I can turn for help. I become despondent and depressed.

All too aware of being an outsider, I feel especially estranged from my family—those who spurned me at such an early age.

So though in the prime of my youth, I feel that my life is useless. I am desperately alone.

And then, something far worse...

One night, now at the age of eleven, I am awakened from sleep with a violent yank.

I gasp.

A rancid rag is thrust into my mouth. I gag. I can't tell whether it is the smell or the taste causing my stomach to wretch. Maybe both.

Straining through the darkness, I see the face of my uncle. I'm confused.

He drags me from my mat into a small corridor at the back of the dwelling. It is cold and I am scared.

At first thought, I assume we are in some kind of danger, perhaps there's a fire or an intruder. But the rag… my uncle… my muffled cries for help…, evidence indicating that I'm the only one at risk.

Stripping me naked in the frigid air, he throws me violently to the ground. With one hand, he pins my flailing fists over my head, while hitting me with the other until I stop thrashing.

Then descending on me like a hungry beast ravaging its helpless prey, he rapes me.

With brute strength my uncle forces himself on me. The frightening pitch of his anger spews into the black night as he curses with vile whispers while assaulting me.

Unaware of my female anatomy, I feel the violation in places with which I'm not familiar—the horror is penetrating to the very core of my being. I scream in agonizing pain, but no one can hear me.

Finally, I collapse beneath the weight of his cruelty.

Then it is over.

He jerks me from the ground and thrusts my garment at me, whispering in harsh tones.

Get up and get dressed. Hurry up!

Wiping the sweat from his upper lip with the back of his hand, he continues barking at me.

Go back inside, and don't speak a word of this to anyone! You understand?

He has finished with me for the night.

I rise from the floor, bruised and bloody, reeking of his smell. Gathering my garment about my shoulders, I start toward the door.

He slaps me hard on the cheek.

My head rocks back as I stagger to catch myself from falling.

Answer me, girl! Did you hear me?

The blow from his fist is a peculiar distraction from the degradation I feel. I answer, sobbing.

Yes, Uncle.

I run quietly out of his presence, slipping outside through another door.

The urge to vomit overtakes me.

Afterward, I just stand still, breathing in the fresh air. I consider whether to run away. But where would I go? I have only distant relatives—those whom I met at my mother's

funeral years ago—those who obviously despise me because
of my scandalous conception. And since, unlike our male
counterparts, young Jewish maidens offer no promise of
future income, they wouldn't welcome one more mouth to
feed, anyway.

I finally drag myself back to my cot, smelling of bile.
An offensive odor but, at least for now, it hides the stench of
rape.

In the quiet aftermath of trauma, I attend a funeral in
my imagination. It is just like the one which had occurred at
my mother's death. All of the sneering relatives are standing
in the periphery of my mind's eye and looking on me with
disgust. I feel the isolation of the dead woman. Unclean.
Unfit to live among others.

My uncle has a habit of saying that I am worthless. He
proved that he was right all along, I am a reproach among
the living. I had feared that I was cast in my mother's mold.
And sure enough, I am...

Naked, ashamed, unclean... just like her.

I wish I were dead.

The rape marks a passage in my childhood from which
I feel there is no return. The last remaining ember of hope is
extinguished from my heart.

My depression now gives way to a desperate fear. Like
a defenseless animal, I spend my days glancing over my

shoulder at the slightest sounds, startling at shadows behind every object. The relentless dread of my uncle's advances threatens me every moment, for I can't erase the frightful images of violation. The more I try to escape them, the more persistently they assault me.

I live in a constant state of terror, knowing that as sure as the morning dawns, the night will come... and with it, the insatiable appetite of his depravity.

Oh, Philip, how it disturbs me to share this dark time in my life with you. The darkest of times. A darkness that terrified me then. But you must hear it so that you will understand all that has happened to me.

Night after night, I lie paralyzed with fear, waiting...

If left alone, fatigue finally surrenders me to the sleep of despair, haunted by my dreams.

But if not, fear stops its clamoring for the night, once the horror has come and gone. My mind gives over more readily, then, to sleep. And all that remains after the routine of rape is an ache in my body that throbs in rhythm with the anguish in my heart.

The injury of my uncle's assault grows inside of me like an infection. A dangerous despair—bordering on rage—simmers deep within. I seethe with resentment and, with nowhere to turn and no one to help, I entertain savage thoughts of revenge.

At last, when I reach the age of sixteen, a man requests my hand in marriage.

I am afraid that my uncle won't release me. And if not for the dowry, he wouldn't. Greed is the only thing that motivates him more than the gratification of his flesh, so he auctions me off to the man with little hesitation.

I am relieved to exchange my uncle's abuse for my husband's demands, mild as they are by comparison.

It isn't long before I discover that what my husband really wants is a son. Having a wife is a mild inconvenience with which he has to cope in order to obtain an heir. Unfortunately, after two years of marriage, I have not conceived.

I suppose I should have suspected it all along, since I'd never become pregnant through all those years of violation. My whole life has been barren, so it stands to reason that my womb would be, too.

Still, it hurt.

It's probably best, I reason. I might have had a daughter, and she would be just like me. Just like my mother.

Avoiding my eyes, he offers me a certificate of divorce.

I can't afford to waste any more time.

Waste time?

Obviously, your womb is dead. I see no reason to continue.

No reason at all?

A lump swells into my throat. Now I look away. But he is anxious to finish with the matter.

I married hoping to have a son.

I know.

I can't afford to keep you here — you'll need to be going.

He waves me away with his hand.

Gathering my things, I set out on foot just as the sun perches itself upon the rooftops at dusk. I hesitate for a moment, realizing that I failed to accept the certificate. But I can't turn back, I'm too humiliated as it is.

As I walk away, my mind reaches back in time… to a day early in my childhood. I remember stumbling across a beautiful blue egg resting on the ground under an olive tree. Picking it up from where it lay, I intended to return it to its nest.

To my dismay, I found that it was empty. A tiny hole in the delicate veneer betrayed the visitation of some villain, whose sharp beak had penetrated it, sucking the precious substance of life right out, leaving behind a hollow shell.

What do I do now, with no home and no husband? I can't go back to my former life. A wave of panic surges inside.

It occurs to me that there is only one alternative to consider besides returning to my uncle's house — the legacy left by my mother. Prostitution, it seems, would be more tolerable than living with him. So I choose the dead woman's disgrace over the shame of my living uncle.

Without a moment's hesitation, I set out for the harlot

house; unaware that this decision will have far greater implications for my life than I could imagine in the present.

Because I am young and reasonably unsullied, the proprietor of the house decides to keep me on reserve in the service of a Roman dignitary. He pays handsomely for exclusive rights to me. Though demeaning, it provides a delicate introduction to what I discover is a cruel and inhumane occupation.

But by the age of 23, I am out on the streets, accepting payment from my first public patron. I quickly discover that I will have to accept a complete disregard for my dignity, as well. It is merely rape for hire.

Smelling of dead fish, the stocky, middle-aged man finishes with me, panting. He lifts his cloak from the floor, huffing with complaint between every breath.

You aren't as lively as the last one.

I pull my mantle up, trying to shield myself from his eyes.

You've still got a few things to learn about men. Tricks of the trade, if you know what I mean.

I'm not in the mood for his crude conversation. I just want him to go. I turn to face the wall. But he keeps rattling on.

Can't really complain about the price, though, since you're the cheapest in the house.

Just go, please.

He offers up one last insult before slipping out the door, leaving me in a heap of anguish and confusion.

Night after night, and from one stranger's bed to another, I suffer through the vulgar fantasies of men with no conscience. I have simply traded one abuse I couldn't stop for another of my own choosing.

I am aware that an even deeper decay has inflicted my soul. I feel as if my spirit is rotting away. Something writhes and twists inside—something unfit for human eyes. And with each intimate encounter, the resentment inside of me festers.

As the days pile up into years, I eventually surrender all hope of ever escaping the prison in which I live. The one faint glimmer of innocence to which I still clung—a remnant from my childhood—is, at last, entirely eclipsed by evil. There isn't a shred of decency remaining in any part of my existence.

One day, many years into the journey, a new darkness seizes hold of me…

A man barges into the dwelling where I have found temporary shelter in exchange for erotic favors. He grips me by the shoulders and wrenches me from the arms of an indifferent stranger, yanking me upright.

In the harsh light, he examines me with disgust. The strain of my occupation has taxed my physical appearance unsparingly. I grab my cloak, trying to hide from his revulsion.

His voice is stern.

Come with me.

I try to wrestle free.

Why me?

Don't bother feigning innocence, harlot.

But what have I done to you?

I struggle frantically with the garment, pulling it awkwardly around my shoulders.

This time, he doesn't answer. Gripping my arm fiercely, he drags me like a tethered goat through the city of Jerusalem.

I have been staying in the city only because business is good during religious holidays. Men frequently attend the festivals without their families, and many of them participate in drunken orgies under the guise of worship while away from home.

I know I can count on their infidelity as a dependable source of income. After all, it isn't difficult to seduce a man whose religion is merely ritual.

Seeing that the temple is our destination, I feel a knot swelling in my throat. I have heard about the Holy Shrine, but have never ventured near. Long ago, I was told that the God of my people is a god whose favor rests only upon men.

I try to resist—to pull away—but the man shoves me forward, and I stumble into the temple courtyard. Gasps and whispers stir. I tug nervously at my cloak, trying to keep myself covered.

Looking around, I see that I'm in the company of the

religious elite. Gawking at me are the respectable men and women of our devout society; and in their expressions I witness all of the horrors of rejection I have always felt, yet now, magnified by the lens of religion.

Feeling like an infected patch of leprosy under inspection by a priest, I sense the prickly daggers of people's disgust piercing my skin and penetrating my heart.

I see, in the sea of faces, a few whom I have been with this week. No names, just faces. They recognize me, as well, for they quickly turn and disappear in the crowd.

The man clutching my arm speaks coldly and evenly, but this time not to me.

Teacher, this woman was caught in adultery; in the very act!

The audience gasps in unison. A cluster of middle-aged women draw back slightly, in order to avoid the possibility of contamination. The men shake their heads with disdain.

I lift my gaze to see if the man caught in adultery has been dragged in behind me.

No. Just as I suspected, I am the only sinner in the arena.

The man continues talking.

In the Law, Moses commands us to stone such women. What do you say?

I am gripped with terror! This must be what became of my mother.

I want to run, but am rooted to the spot with fear.

A heavy silence falls over the courtyard. Anticipation hangs in the air.

I search the crowd with my eyes, looking for the man he calls Teacher. I am astonished to discover how ordinary he looks… But more astonishing still, he is looking at me, searching my eyes.

He studies my face, causing my heart to burn scarlet and blush up onto my cheeks. But he doesn't say a word.

The grip on my arm tightens. My captor's knuckles knot up. I feel the tension coursing through his fist and into my flesh. He is unresponsive, though I wince with discomfort, distracted as he is with every moment that passes in silence. I begin to wonder if I am the victim of a conflict that has nothing to do with me.

Then, in that strained moment, the most peculiar thing…

The Teacher lowers his gaze and stoops down to write something in the sand.

The crowd stirs restlessly; their focus shifting from me to him.

Was it intentional?

My captor, incensed with the Teacher's response, demands an answer.

Did you hear me? I asked you what you have to say.

This time, the strain in his voice betrays the unnerving effect that the Teacher's odd behavior is having upon him.

Another minute crawls by. The Teacher lifts his gaze and examines the man's countenance—looking for something.

After a moment, he looks again at me—a look I've never seen. What is it… in his eyes? Sadness? Yes, perhaps, but not only sadness. It's a sorrow mingled with longing. As if he is looking at the object of his unrequited devotion.

I feel his gaze penetrate almost through me; into the very depths of my being, searching the tortured regions of my heart with which he seems already familiar. And strange as it seems, I feel the chaos churning inside of me turn to calm—like a tranquil sea once the storm subsides.

Is it possible that this is what mercy looks like?

I'm confused. It seems to me that his actions aren't consistent with his judicial obligation. He is, after all, a teacher of the Law, and I am in violation of it. I am guilty; and, according to the Law, I stand condemned.

He lowers his gaze again and continues writing in the sand with his finger. His face is stern, a look which I interpret could mean my end is near.

I shudder, imagining that these people are going to pound the life out of me. It causes my stomach to wrench with grief. An acrid taste stings the back of my throat, and tears well up, brimming over in hot, salty streams, leaving red streaks of shame to stain my face.

Then, just as suddenly as he had stooped, the Teacher straightens up. Surveying the crowd, he starts speaking.

Whoever among you is without sin...

He pauses, raises his hand, and with a slow, sweeping gesture, motions across the throng. Then he stops, resting his eyes upon the man at my side—his hand, palm up, open before him.

The man's eyebrows arch. He is being singled out.

...throw the first stone.

The Teacher locks his gaze on the man until, at last, he lets go of my arm. Deliberately, then, he glances across the crowd, looking into the face of every person, one by one.

Appearing embarrassed and uncomfortable, they shuffle their feet and turn away to avoid his eyes.

Finally, the Teacher kneels down again and resumes his writing.

I wait in strained silence as, one at a time, they begin to walk away, dropping their rocks as they go. The sound echoes through my head, one muffled thud falling on the other.

Whispering behind cupped hands, a few young people hang back, waiting to see what will happen. When my captor himself slips away, they, too, leave the courtyard.

I am free.

We are alone, the Teacher and me. He is still stooped down and drawing in the dust.

I swipe at my swollen eyes and sniff back the remaining tears. I don't know this man. I can't let myself be vulnerable.

Eventually, he looks up and studies my face again. Straightening up and brushing the dust from his hands, he walks toward me. I avert my gaze thinking that he might interpret the looseness of my robe as an invitation. After all, he knows what I am.

He stops directly in front of me, looking into my face.

I feel strangely unashamed and return his look.

His voice is softer now, gentler than before.

Woman, where are they? Is there no one left to condemn you?

He had been kneeling right there, waiting for someone to throw the first stone. In fact, he'd granted them a peculiar kind of permission to carry out the execution.

I finally gather enough courage to answer.

It seems they have all left, Rabbi.

He sighs, as if relieved. Smiling, he reaches to squeeze my hand in his.

Then neither do I condemn you.

I am simply astonished. I find this whole situation inconceivable. First, he runs off the religious people, then, he stays to speak with me, a harlot. I cannot help asking.

Why?

Humored by my response, his smile widens, crinkling the skin around his eyes.

A long, comfortable silence passes as his eyes search for connection.

Finally, he nods, gesturing toward the city.

You are free to go. But leave behind the sin that brought you here.

His words resonate somewhere inside of me, as if just by speaking them, he dispelled the prophecy of doom that had hung over my life since the beginning.

Overwhelmed with emotion and an amazing sense of peace, I open my mouth to speak, to thank him for taking the time to talk to me, and for treating me, undeserving as I am, with dignity. But words won't come. Tears well up, instead.

Someone calls from a distance, interrupting.

Jesus!

The Teacher looks in the man's direction, answering.

Over here.

He turns to look at me once more. Pointing toward the place where he had stooped—at the writing in the sand—he nods.

Then he walks away.

Now, I am alone with myself and feeling strangely serene.

I linger awhile. The silence sounds reassuring.

Advancing to where he first bent down, I recall his peculiar behavior.

An old priest on his way out of the temple stops beside me. His voice creaks with age.

Are you the woman of whom the authorities tried to make a spectacle?

Yes, I'm Mary, of Magdala.

I hear that the Nazarene silenced the fray.

He smiles, a sly grin, indicating his approval of the Teacher's actions.

Yes, he did.

I've heard him teach, you know.

He looks at me, anticipating a reaction. Then he continues.

I've seen him heal people, too—as if it is nothing for a man to restore sight to the blind.

He is silent for a moment, contemplating, perhaps, the events about which he has spoken. He continues, at last.

The authorities say nothing good can come out of Nazareth, but it looks as if they were wrong.

His eyes follow my gaze to the script in the sand.

Can you read it?

I hadn't yet acquired the learning. I respond modestly.

No, I can't.

Looks like a list of some sort — but a strange one, indeed.

He frowns, twisting his head to get a better angle. He begins reading out loud.

Fear, depression, despair, bitterness, barrenness...

I gasp!

His head snaps up to meet my gaze.

Does this sound familiar to you?

I don't know...

I recognize that the words describe me perfectly, but I feel suddenly vulnerable.

Awareness begins to dawn on the old priest's face.

Woman, I think I recognize what these are!

I start to back away, uncertain what he might say.

If I'm right...

I turn to run, but he grabs me by the shoulders.

I try to yank away.

You're scaring me!

I cover my ears, but he says it anyway.

They're demons!

No!

Shaking me gently, he demands that I listen.

Don't be afraid… Don't you see what has happened? He has set you free, Mary. You mustn't fear.

I can't help it! They're the souls of the wicked dead!

At that, tears begin streaming down my face.

Poor girl, you've suffered so much. Jesus must have seen right through your tortured heart. He saw what was plaguing you, and he has made it right.

I can't stop sobbing. My strength is sapped.

Don't cry, Mary. They're gone.

The old man reaches for me and I fall into his embrace. He holds me while I cry—cradling me like a child in his arms, rocking me gently back and forth—as a father would do. Finally, the tears subside.

He brushes a strand of hair from my face with a wrinkled hand, wiping the moisture from my cheek. His tenderness touches something unfamiliar in me. He gestures at the writing in the sand.

Mary, look at how he did it! One by one, he called them out. As he named each one, each one was bound and you were set free. Seven were named, daughter, and you are free. Do you understand?

I am staggered by it all.

Seven of them?

Yes, but there is no need to worry, he drove them out… for good!

I can't help asking.

Why would he do that for me? I'm guilty of the wrong I was accused of.

The old priest's expressive eyes glisten as he speaks.

Those who accused you have their demons, as well.

It's almost more than I can grasp, but I feel a strange sensation pulsing through me. I suspect it could be hope.

He steadies me to stand on my own, speaking softly.

I must be on my way.

Please, wait with me awhile. I'm not sure what I should do.

Do whatever the Teacher told you.

You mean, stop pleasuring men?

Yes.

He looks sad.

And stop destroying yourself.

But that's how I make a living.

He shakes his head slowly.

That isn't living, dear one.

He turns to leave, then pauses a moment.

Messiah will show you the way.

I stall.

I just wish I had had the chance to thank him.

He smiles and nods.

You will, my dear. You will.

As I watch him fade into the distance, I suddenly remember that the Teacher knelt twice.

I look down, searching the ground for the second script. My heart begins to race. There it is!

I shout at the priest.

Come back! I can't read.

But he is out of earshot.

I stoop down, just as he had, and squint through grateful tears.

There in the dust is the very sequence of symbols you observed on my pendant…

Like you, Philip, the symbols had a curious effect on me. It was as if a familiar chord had been plucked in my soul from some long-forgotten melody.

The first of the five symbols—the arrow pointing downward as if descending from heaven to earth…

…signifies his coming.

Jesus came.

All of the devout people present that day thought he came because religion demanded it; but I know in my heart that wasn't the reason. It was me he was after.

And if he came for a hopeless harlot like me, then there is no doubt: he will come for you, too.

Your servant always,
Mary of Magdala

THE SECOND PARCHMENT..., WRITTEN IN THE
LATE SUMMER OF THE SAME YEAR, A.D. 35...

GREETINGS, PHILIP,

My heart grows heavier with every day that passes without word from you.

Your father stopped by the synagogue in Capernaum two days ago. I sensed the desperation in his voice.

Mary, I haven't received any news from my son. Has anyone here heard anything?

No, but we've been praying for him day and night.

What about your letter — was it delivered?

I'm not certain. The proprietor accepted it, but told the courier that Philip hasn't been seen in quite awhile.

He wrung his hands anxiously as the information sunk in. I tried to encourage him with the news of another attempt to reach you.

Julius, the Roman centurion, has enlisted the support of some soldiers whom he trusts. They have a much broader reach than we do as civilians.

He is a good man and a loyal friend. But the situation is getting worse. Herod considers any follower of Jesus an enemy of his.

It's all very political, isn't it?

He nodded, continuing.

There are those with a thirst for power which can never be satisfied, Mary. And Herod's family history is insanely violent in that regard. You know it was his father who ordered the slaughter of the infants in Bethlehem when news of Jesus' birth reached him. They are men with no conscience.

Chuza, do you remember your first encounter with Messiah?

His eyebrows arched. He seemed curious that I would bring it up.

Of course.

Your son's life was hanging in the balance then, too. If my memory serves me correctly, you ran from Capernaum to Cana seeking Messiah's help.

Because I'd heard he had the power to heal.

But when you got to Cana, you hesitated. Am I right?

I just wasn't sure that he would receive me because of my position, being an officer in Herod's court. Herod had wrongfully imprisoned John the Baptist, who happened to be related to Messiah. And remember, Mary, I was also afraid that if Herod found out, my whole family would be at risk.

But desperation won out. You found him and begged him to come to Capernaum with you.

Any father in my position would have done the same.

He gazed off. His expression betrayed the fresh experience of emotion he felt from so long ago.

In a moment, he spoke again, shaking his head in amazement.

He healed my son from right there, where he stood—a distance of 27 miles.

He paused and turned to look at me again.

He was so attentive, Mary, so compassionate. Did I ever tell you that before I left, he embraced me—you know, the way Hebrew men embrace each other?

I brought it up to remind you, Chuza, that just as you trusted Messiah with Philip's life then, you can trust him now.

But Mary, I never told Philip the truth about that incident.

What?!

Grief etched your father's face.

He was too young to remember much about it, and I was trying to protect him. I thought he'd be safer, not knowing, with Herod's disposition as it is. But now that Philip is a grown man, I fear that he doesn't know the truth about Jesus.

I placed my hand on his shoulder.

Chuza, I tried to tell him.

When? What are you talking about?

The night of our arrest, Philip had asked about the meaning of the symbols on my pendant.

His brow knotted.

What symbols?

Those engraved on my necklace.

Yes, I've seen them… somewhere.

Julius made them for us, at first, to help us identify each other in the presence of the opposition. Later, after the authorities became aware, they became a symbol of our courage.

Yes, that's it! And the authorities think it's a secret code signifying underground activity. They find it threatening.

So I've heard. And Julius has risked more than merely his position in the army. There are men in power seeking to find out who continues spreading the story of Jesus this way so they can put an end to him, but they don't know who the craftsman is. I doubt they would ever suspect it is a Roman soldier!

I never knew he possessed such skill, I doubt anyone else does, either.

Chuza, I was about to tell Philip about Jesus, when the soldiers broke in. That is why I'm so desperate to reach him. That's what my letter was about.

Keep trying, Mary. He is at great risk, not knowing.

That is how our conversation went, Philip, so now you see that it was your father's fear of Herod that compelled him to send you away, while you were still young, to your mother's family in Caesarea. It was for your own protection.

Chuza feared that you would be in danger if word got out about your healing, because Herod couldn't risk any further indictment against himself. It wasn't long after that, that he had John the Baptist murdered and the people were up in arms over it.

Grieving your absence, your mother came to despise Herod. And out of gratitude for your healing, she courageously joined Messiah's mission supporting his ministry from her personal means.

Joanna became my close friend and her untimely death brought me much sorrow. Her last words were of you, and her heartfelt desire that I share with you the meaning of our mission.

So, for this reason also, I feel pressed to continue writing to you—sharing my testimony—while there is still time.

Do you remember where I left off? It was in the moments following my encounter with Jesus at the Temple in Jerusalem…

Still in the courtyard, I am bent down, staring at the scribbling in the sand left there by the Teacher.

My mind reaches back through time. I cannot deny the impulse to connect this new revelation of demon-possession with the desperation I have known for so long.

When did I first sense their presence? That terrible darkness and oppression that settled over me?

Was I a mere child, or a young woman?

Am I somehow responsible, or was it my uncle's fault?

Did they overtake me all at once, or one at a time?

I ponder over it, struggling to make sense of my past. Realizing that the answers aren't easy ones, one thing becomes clear—my life will be different from now on. The

Teacher delivered me; the demons are gone! And though I don't understand it all, I know that the source of my misery has been banished, for I feel an indescribable peace.

I realize that I should leave Jerusalem right away. But where should I go?

Prostitution is out of the question now; the old priest is right, that is no way to live. But returning to my uncle's house... The thought of it overwhelms me.

How will I support myself? The only money-making skill I possess is death to me.

I wish I had asked the Teacher if he has followers in the city with which I could stay temporarily. On second thought, they wouldn't want to be associated with a known harlot.

I swallow hard and head back to Magdala.

The closer I get to my uncle's house, the more I agonize over living under the roof of a man who had held me captive to his depravity for so many years.

Before long, I am at the door to his dwelling. Weak with fear, I consider walking away. But I have nowhere else to turn.

I give up the debate and knock.

The door flings open, and a sickening wave of dread floods my heart. My uncle looks shocked to see me after so many years. But I detect something sinister in his voice as he announces me to his wife.

Look who's here!

From inside, I hear my aunt gasp faintly.

My uncle steps aside, and I squeeze by him,

uncomfortably close. He slams the door and stands in front of it, leaving me feeling trapped.

He has the first word.

Why did you come back? Are you pregnant?

No.

Tension swells in the room as we stare at each other for a moment. It suddenly occurs to me that he might have wanted to ask me that question many times over the years, when it could have implicated him.

He presses.

Then what do you want?

I have no place to stay; this is the only home I have ever known.

I want more than anything to run out the door and go anywhere… other than here.

He laughs, cynically.

Is that what you think this is — your home?

His words still hold the power to wound me.

My aunt breaks in timidly.

Please, let her stay. I could use her help around the house.

His gaze is fastened on me, but he directs his rebuke at her.

Be quiet, woman! I'll handle this.

There is no mistaking the threat in his tone. I know precisely what he means. I feel something ignite within me, flaming up on my face.

Struggling to maintain my composure, I try to reason with him.

The truth is, I have given up prostitution, and I'm here because I desperately want to live a different life.

His eyes narrow with suspicion.

Why would you give it up now, after all this time?

I met this man…

He laughs… loudly, and sarcastically, stopping me mid-sentence. Then, in a high-pitched voice, he mocks me.

I met a man. Well, of course you did — you're a whore!

I fight the urge to slap him, clenching my fists tightly, my nails digging into my palms.

He jabs a finger in my direction.

Your reputation is beyond repair; even my good name can't fix the mess you've made! You might as well forget the man. No one would have you after what you've done.

You don't understand. I was talking about a different kind of man.

He tosses his hands in the air in an exaggerated gesture. Then he turns to open the door again, shouting over his shoulder to my aunt.

She is numb to his insults.

I study her with sympathy; a person who was long ago stripped of her dreams. She is a shell of a woman who survives on the meager existence he allots her.

As she helps me settle into the corner of the tiny room at the back of the dwelling, I try to assure her.

I won't cause trouble for you, I promise.

We embrace, tearfully. I sense that my presence is a comfort to her.

Unfortunately, my uncle isn't gone long. I hurry to bed,

avoiding any further confrontation. I don't want to be here, and I dread what lies ahead.

I simply hope I survive this.

In the middle of the night, I am startled awake by something. It isn't yet morning, and I don't remember dreaming...

I sense evil in the room. Suddenly, I realize that my uncle is standing over my cot, just as in the days of old.

Though facing the other direction, I can smell his foul breath and it sends shivers down my spine. I feel the tiny hairs on the back of my neck stand up in self-defense.

I'm not sure what I should do, but I don't want to be at a disadvantage, so I sit up and whirl around to face him.

It startles him slightly.

Confronting him, I whisper loudly.

What are you doing here?

Shut up! You'll wake your aunt.

Then tell me what it is you want.

He reaches for my arm, the way he used to years ago.

I'll tell you what you need to know.

I yank away.

Don't touch me!

Anger flares up on his face.

I'll do whatever I want, you wretch.

He reaches forcefully for the edge of my garment. But just as he attempts to rip it off, I slap him hard on the face.

He isn't used to me fighting back. Now he is full of rage.

I jump to my feet, shouting at the top of my voice.

Get away from me!

Grabbing me by the hair, he forces me down on the mat again. Landing flat on my back, I manage one fierce kick to his groin. He doubles over in pain, howling like a dog.

Leaping up, I run out of the house and back into the night. I have no thought about where I'm going, I'm just running from him.

Once I'm a safe distance from the dwelling, I stop — bending over to catch my breath. In that moment, I realize that I know of only one other place I can go — to the house of prostitution.

Once inside, I collapse, my heart pounding wildly. One of the hired girls jumps out of her cot to tend to me. She stays with me through the night, listening as I weep and recount my heartache.

The next few days are the darkest of my life. I cannot return to my uncle, and the proprietor of the harlot house insists that I can stay only as long as I bring in business. I exhaust every excuse I can think of; but his patience finally wears thin, and he gives me an ultimatum.

You will work tonight, or you are back on the streets!

ꕙꕊꗋꕊ

Out of desperation, I concede. I resume my prior occupation, only this time with the words of the Teacher echoing through my mind—*Sin no more.*

It doesn't take long before I'm sinning more than ever. I find that living with guilt is far worse than living with demons. It would be easier to blame my circumstances than to have to bear my own shame. I am now filled with self-loathing.

Hardening myself against the pangs of my conscience, I become embittered and apathetic.

One night, while hired out to one of the holy men in the city, I find myself so repulsed that I cannot perform. I've entertained his type many times through the years, but ever since the temple incident, I'm nauseated at the sight of them.

These men—who carry themselves with an air of superiority in the light of day, and in the eyes of others— grovel in the dark with the very ones they condemn, in order to satisfy their baser cravings. Yet no one suspects their duplicity. I often wonder who it is the people think wears down the footpath between here and the synagogue.

Angry at my lack of enthusiasm, he becomes abusive. He sits up, threatening me.

You either get lively, or I'll be sure you don't get hired again!
I lash back.
I can't, you disgust me!

What are you talking about, Woman? You're the one who's up for hire.

And you're a hypocrite!

He hits me hard across the cheek.

Watch your words, you whore.

My voice is trembling, but I won't back down.

You're all just alike — you holy men.

How dare you!

A man, just like you, dragged me half-naked into the temple courts in Jerusalem recently. I saw you there. You saw what a spectacle he made of me.

He frowns. It's obvious I have struck a sensitive place in his hardened heart.

He stands and reaches for his mantle. Troubling thoughts knit his brow, and his words betray his concern.

What does that have to do with me?

I resent you; you are as guilty as I am. How I wish the tables would turn so that I could expose all of you!

My words startle him.

You recognize me?

Of course I do, Simon the Pharisee. I saw you there.

A grave look falls over his face, and a slight tremor creeps into his voice.

What do you want for your silence?

What could you possibly give me, a reputation perhaps?

He reaches inside his cloak and removes a beautiful flask of perfume from a pouch tucked inside. It is a vial — pure alabaster. Exquisite.

It is very valuable. Take it, and leave me be. You will never see me again.

He thrusts it at me, and turns to slither out the door like a serpent — secretly — fleeing under the cover of night.

Recognizing its value, I quickly sew the small vial into the hem of my garment before the proprietor comes and catches me with it. After all, I'm not cheating him, he got his due. I'm the one who has been cheated all along.

The next day, I have to work the marketplace. We take turns drumming up the evening's business by our presence in public during the day.

Rounding a corner on the narrow street, I notice a crowd gathered around a man who is telling a lively story. I edge near to listen.

He has heard rumors that in Nain, a city just a few miles away, a man has been raised from the dead. The event has caused an uproar in nearby Nazareth, because the one who performed the miracle is a native of that city. A carpenter, of all things.

I gasp audibly, remembering the words of the old priest.

He called the Teacher a Nazarene.

The man continues breathlessly, explaining that the Nazarene is headed this way on his return trip to Capernaum.

Could it be him?

Gossip bounces about the marketplace all day. Some say

the miracle-worker has turned for Jerusalem. Others say he has bypassed Magdala and cut across Cana to Capernaum. Still others say that he was overtaken at Tiberius and is being delayed by the authorities there.

From the hem of my garment, the weight of the alabaster vial tugs at my conscience—I have betrayed the one who rescued me from the very evil to which I've now returned. I'm like a dog eating his own vomit.

Anxious over the man's report, I fear that this miracle-worker might be him—and at the same time, I fear that it might not. Either way, I could never face him. He would know what I have done; just like he knew about the demons.

But perhaps, he won't even remember me.

Too numb to think, yet afraid to return to the house without work, I roam the streets aimlessly.

As I approach the crest of a hill, I see a mob of people moving my way. I turn to take a different route. Assuming that the crowd will stay on the main path, I slip into the shadows of a nearby alley. Wishing to become invisible, I lean back against a building, my head resting against its side.

The crowd flows over the hill and turns, heading toward me. I just hope they will pass quickly.

I don't know whether it is intuition, or what, but something grips me as they approach. I am riveted to their faces, powerless to wrestle my gaze from them. And he is there; in the midst of the crowd.

Suddenly, our eyes meet.

He looks directly at me, and though many press against

him, I am the only person he sees. I cannot move my gaze from him. And just as I had feared, I can see in his eyes that he knows what I have done. A sense of failure and wrenching heartache overwhelm me and tears spring to my eyes.

I turn to look away. I just wish he hadn't come—not to find me like this.

I rip myself from the wall, gathering my garment up, and run as fast as I can.

Stumbling into my room, I fall face first onto the cot, burying myself in its yeasty smell. Remorse pours in a torrent of tears. I wail loudly and without restraint.

I wanted things to be different.

I wanted so desperately to live right

I couldn't even muster the strength to thank him, much less to stop sinning.

Convicted at once by my own words, I sit bolt upright, my tears dammed up behind a sudden determination. *Though I have failed him, still, I should thank him. I had never felt hope like he was able to show me. I had never felt that sense of freedom that he gave me. I am so thankful; I must tell him! It's not too late! He's still in the city, somewhere!*

I scurry to my feet, grab my shawl, and run out the door and into the street.

A man passes me from the opposite direction, and I grab his arm.

Can you tell me where the Nazarene rabbi went?

Let go of me.

Please, is he staying here in Magdala?

He's at the house of a Pharisee. What is it to you?

Which Pharisee?

Simon. Who else?

Of course! The most prominent man of the city always hosts the meal for the visiting rabbi. He has to uphold his image of distinction, regardless of his personal feelings about the Teacher.

I start toward Simon's house, resolved to express my gratitude, though I'm not sure how I'll get in.

Yes, of course! The vial!

In the thick shade of a large tree just outside of Simon's dwelling, I bend over, ripping at the stitches in my skirt. Retrieving the priceless bottle of perfume from my hem, I hug it close, feeling a surge of confidence.

A servant stands in the doorway, menacing anyone who tries to enter.

I approach him boldly.

I'm here to see Simon.

I doubt you would be welcome here. In any case, Simon is dining with the rabbi from Nazareth.

I open my hand, revealing the treasure.

I've come to return this.

His eyes widen.

Does this belong to Simon?

Surely you recognize it.

He holds out his hand.

Give it to me, then. I'll make sure he gets it when the evening is over.

No, I must give it to him myself.

He hesitates a moment. I hold my breath. Then, with a quick jerk of his head, he invites me to follow.

I nearly lose my breath when I see him. *Jesus.*

He's reclining at a table, with his back toward me. He's so near, I could touch him. Leaning on his left elbow, his feet are extended behind him—just within reach.

I'm certain he doesn't know that I'm in the room. But Simon does. He startles at the sight of me. A reasonable reaction, considering what I said last night about wanting to expose him.

I raise the vial so he can see it, thinking it will buy me some time to figure out how to address the Teacher. Simon has no idea that I'm here to see Jesus—to thank him. This time, I won't miss my chance.

I let my gaze fall back onto the lean frame in front of me. My eyes mist over as I recall how I had first seen him, stooping down to write in the dirt. He had shocked us all with his unconventional behavior.

I clear my throat to speak—to say his name; but just like before, my voice sticks in my throat, swelling into an aching knot. The words won't come!

I look frantically around the room. Every man present is glaring at me, except the Teacher, who still hasn't noticed my arrival.

Rattled by their obvious disdain, I become overwhelmed with emotion. I can't think. I am so flustered I begin to tremble.

What am I doing here?

I can't remember why I thought that I deserve the opportunity to speak with him.

Suddenly, the knot in my throat dissolves. Without warning, tears burst through with unexpected force. I struggle, trying to regain my composure. I feel so reckless having barged in here to thank the Teacher. My coming like this will only put his reputation at risk. If I venture to speak with him, it will only humiliate him. After all, each man here knows who I am.

If I leave now, before he sees me, he will never know I was here...

Quickly, I duck and start to back out of the door.

But what's this? I notice there are mud splotches on Jesus' feet.

I am aghast! Is this my fault? Not only have I risked smearing his reputation, now I've muddied his feet with the dirt I've carried in on my garment.

I glance down at my skirt to see the dirt on my hem. There isn't any.

How, then, could his feet be muddy? The servant who brought me in would have washed his feet when he arrived...

Suddenly, everything becomes clear. I raise my eyes again, confronting Simon silently. Jesus' feet were not washed. They were still dirty when he reclined at the table. When my tears fell on his feet, mingling with the dirt, they turned to mud.

I know it to be an intentional show of disrespect; for Simon has refused the Teacher the most basic rite of Hebrew hospitality.

His arrogance causes me to burn with indignation.

I drop to my knees, furious. I won't leave him like this. Though I don't have the courage to thank him, I won't leave him to the insult of this pious fraud.

Reaching inside my shawl, I let loose my braid; and in defiance of his refusal to dignify Jesus with a towel, I bend down and wipe his feet with the only part of me that is undefiled — my hair.

The nearness, the realness, of him is overwhelming, causing my anger to melt into appreciation once more. I've never touched a man's skin voluntarily, and never with pure intentions. Remembering the gentle way he spoke to me, the way he rescued me from the oppression of demons, my heart feels like it could burst. I lean over and kiss his feet out of gratitude.

Then, on an impulse, I break the vial.

In a spontaneous outpouring of my heart, I release the expensive ointment upon the only one worthy of its contents—rubbing it tenderly into his calloused soles. If this is all I ever do again, it will be enough.

All at once, the room feels rife with tension. I lift my gaze to discover that the men around the table are staring at me with disgust; although Jesus has not yet acknowledged me with so much as a glance. I am discomfited by his silence after this lavish display of affection.

I feel like a spectacle...

Suddenly, he speaks. Shattering the uncomfortable silence and startling me. But his words do not deliver me from my now awkward demonstration, for they aren't directed at me.

Simon, I have something to say to you.

What did I expect? How foolish of me to hope that he would actually say something to me.

I blush with humiliation.

Simon answers with an edge of sarcasm in his voice.

Say it, Teacher.

A certain money-lender had two debtors; one owed five hundred dollars, and the other fifty. When they were unable to repay, he graciously forgave them both. Which of them therefore will love him more?

Though crumpled on the floor at his feet, hair hanging loose, and tears streaming down my face, I'm invisible to him.

Is he so embarrassed that he's acting as if I don't exist?

Simon answers the Teacher smugly.

I suppose the one whom he forgave more.

You are correct.

I sense that Simon is thinking that if the Teacher is truly who he says he is, he would never allow someone like me to touch him. Now that the evidence against him is destroyed, he no longer feels at risk. I'm afraid he's going to try to inflict an even greater humiliation upon Jesus because of what I've done.

So, Simon…

The Teacher resumes speaking, his tone slightly altered, lathered with tenderness.

Do you see this woman?

What? Does he mean me? I lift my head to see.

Compassion pours from his eyes as he turns and looks at me.

When I entered your house, you gave me no water for my feet. But she has wet my feet with her tears.

He reaches with his hand to brush one gently from my cheek.

And, Simon, she wiped my dirty feet with her hair.

His voice resonates with gratitude. His eyes never leave me, yet he still addresses his host.

You gave me no kiss, no affectionate greeting. But she, since the time she came in, has not ceased to kiss my feet. And though you did not anoint my head with oil…

He takes my trembling hand in his and gently pries it open to expose the remaining portion of the broken vial.

She has anointed my feet with costly perfume; in fact, with everything she has.

Simon begins to squirm. This is not what he had planned. He senses that the tables are turning and he is suddenly on trial. Having intentionally withheld his hospitality, he is now fighting the embarrassment he had intended as an insult.

But the Teacher hasn't finished yet.

For this reason I say to you, Simon, her sins…

He pauses, sighing deeply. I realize, from the heaviness in his voice, that he, too, feels the weight of my sin.

Her sins, which are many…

His eyes probe the depths of my heart. He wants me to know that he knows everything. I feel him gently expose the darkness inside of me, but somehow I know I am safe with him.

…They are all forgiven. For, Simon, her heart is consumed with love.

Oddly, I feel only peace that he knows what I have done. I am filled with gratitude; how desperately I had wanted to stop sinning.

Turning, and looking again at Simon, Jesus' eyes are saddened.

But Simon, any man who feels little need of forgiveness will also find very little room in his heart to love.

The room erupts into chaos! The religious men are appalled at this! How dare he come into this righteous man's house and compare him to a prostitute?

Jesus, ignoring the clamor, turns back to me.

You have honored my Father by honoring me. You may go in peace.

But Rabbi, I have nowhere to go.

He rises from the floor, and thanks Simon for the food.

Extending his hand to me, he helps me up and asks me to join him. As we walk out of the dwelling and into the street, he begins telling me things that are almost too wonderful to hear. Jesus has a way of explaining things that clears up all the confusion and relieves all the heartache. He tells me that just as he had come for me that day at the temple, he has come to Magdala, knowing that, by now, I would have discovered a challenging truth. And he is right, I have. I am powerless in my struggle against sin. But knowing him, being near him, seems to provide all that I need in order to overcome.

It is both a shock and a relief to hear him explain that being a prostitute doesn't remove me further from God than does any other sin—however slight. Yet, he insists that having the desire to do all the right things will never mend my past or prevent the mistakes I will make in the future. I listen intently as he informs me that I cannot do anything to make myself whole. However he can, and he will.

I'm not quite certain what he means by all of this, but I think I understand that I will have to rely on him to do for me what I cannot do for myself. He says it is the reason he came.

He finishes our conversation with two small, but powerful words.

Trust me.

And I intend to do just that.

Within three year's time, my intention to live by those two significant words is tested.

I had seen it coming—the deadly threat of jealous men in power—but I couldn't forestall its occurring.

I follow him, sobbing, as he staggers up a barren hillside outside the holy city. There, under the scorching sun, they impale him on the crossbeam they forced him to drag up with him.

I collapse on the ground beside him, hiding my face in the folds of my skirt, as the soldier's hammer falls heavily on the iron spikes that pierce his flesh. Though my hands are cupped tightly over my ears, I still hear the blows ring out morbidly above the muffled roar of the mob.

Gasping in horror, I cringe at the blood that spurts onto my face, reeling with nausea at the sight of the pain contorting his.

I feel each blow as forcefully as if it had pierced my own soul.

No words can describe the horror of this scene. Messiah's execution is crueler than my heart can bear. Yet I can't leave him.

I stay near, huddled with the other women, sobbing, trembling, begging first one man, then another, to rescue him the way he rescued us. But most are here to mock him, as does that cross—that hideous cross—holding him there, helplessly suspended between heaven and earth.

Before the end comes, just as the sun reaches its peak, an eerie darkness suddenly swallows us. And Jesus cries out like a child in the night.

My God! My God! Why have you forsaken me?

The sound of his voice shatters our hearts, as it echoes through the gloom, and into the still silence of eternity.

Finally, he bows his head in surrender, whispering.

Abba, it is finished. Into your hands I entrust my spirit.

As he exhales his last breath, dropping his chin to his chest, a soldier rips open the flesh of his side with a spear, raining blood and water on the rocks beneath him, while the earth shudders in response.

Jesus' life has ended...

I know this as if I had always known it: He has ended in thirst, so that I might never be thirsty. He has finished his mission in abandonment, so that I will never be alone. He has surrendered to the grave, so that I might overcome in life.

And though I am the one who deserves to die, he sacrificed himself to rescue me.

I trust you understand now what the second symbol on my pendant represents…

Jesus died.

He was punished for sins that he did not commit. The sins were ours.

That is the reason he came… to die. He took our place; he rescued us.

My hope is that you won't refuse to take hold of the life that his death has made possible. It is something to which only you can give an answer.

Your servant,
Mary Magdalene

THE THIRD OF FIVE LETTERS... WRITTEN IN THE
FALL OF A.D. 35...

MY DEAR PHILIP,

I asked Julius to see if your name has appeared on any
of the Roman prison rosters. I refuse to give up searching
for you; though it has been so long since I last saw you. I'm
afraid my opportunities may soon come to an end. But I
won't give up, not while there's still hope.

Your father's faith remains a secret to the Roman
government. But, because your mother was identified as one
of us before her death, it's likely that they will assume that
you, too, are a follower of *The Way*.

This puts you in grave danger.

A recent conversation with Julius only confirms my fears.

*The authorities are continuing their aggressive advance against
Messiah's movement. They think they will eventually put an end to it.*

I questioned him.

*Do they think it will muzzle the controversy concerning his
crucifixion?*

Not really. Their part in his execution never has troubled them. But the fact that his death didn't put an immediate end to his influence does worry them. Messiah's following has, instead, only gained momentum through the years.

He is correct about the opposition. But for those of us who loved him, Jesus' murder had been more than troubling. Indeed, on the day that he died, our hope was crucified along with him.

For until then, we had believed that he was the promised one …the Messiah. It seemed obvious to us, after it was over, that we must have been gravely mistaken.

Journey back there with me, Philip…

It is just after Messiah's death…

For three days we've been sitting here, staring numbly at the face of a tomb, wondering what went wrong. Our spirits are withering in the silence of his grave.

As disturbed as we are over where we should go from here and what we should do now, we realize that we can't return to our former way of life. We are different people—all of us—as a result of being with Jesus for the past three years. Being in his presence daily has changed us profoundly.

There was something so contagious about Jesus—an infectious joy, a thrilling sense of anticipation, and a clear understanding of his purpose here that impacted all of us, both as individuals, and as an intimate community. It had been so easy to share in his enthusiasm, getting caught up in the momentum of his mission.

We had watched him every moment and followed his every move, wanting more than anything to be just like him—wanting to share in the tenderness of his healing ministry, in the power he had over the evil spirits, in the energy he exuded in his teaching, and in the amazing intimacy of his own relationship with Abba, particularly when he prayed. None of us would ever forget the awe we experienced when we first heard him pray.

In light of all of this—and especially for someone, like myself, who has been rescued from a lifetime of evil influences—it seems impossible to us that the Jesus who had offered us so much hope for the future, so much insight into the past, and so much joy for the present is now lying stone cold in a borrowed tomb.

We can't make any sense of it. We can't eat or sleep, either. And we certainly can't put our fears to rest. Our remaining strength is poured out with our tears.

The desperation each of us feels is very personal. I catch myself muttering words without thinking.

I'll never look into his eyes again, or hear his laughter.

I'll never hear him sing, or see him smile.

I'll never again hear him say my name.

Every thought of him sweeps me up into a new dimension of grief; and with each, a fresh wave of tears.

I say his name.

Jesus...

And I recall his gentle voice answering.

Mary...

Only Jesus could speak my name that way.

Just a few nights earlier he had done so... just before the end...

On that particular occasion—just days before the crucifixion—we were to stay in the home of Martha and her sister, another woman named Mary. I had been troubled all day prior to our going there because this is the Mary with whom the Lord enjoyed a very special friendship. I was a little envious, I suppose, and he sensed it. He always knew.

Mary is a young widow—then, in her early twenties—vibrant, innocent, and full of charisma. Her laughter reminds me of running water, so refreshing. And her eyes sparkle when she laughs, just like the reflection of the sun off a bubbling brook.

From the very beginning, Mary and Jesus shared a unique connection. It's as if they had an understanding of each other that the rest of us didn't. She seemed to grasp the meaning of his words in a way that few ever did.

It had been an emotional day for me already. Ever since Jesus raised Mary's brother from the dead, we had been trying to stay out of sight. That unforgettable miracle incited the religious leaders against him, resulting in death threats that continued to filter down to us from the ranks of the highest officials.

We could tell that Messiah was taking these matters seriously, for he seemed pensive about the approaching Passover Feast—the most prominent Jewish celebration. He kept talking about laying down his life for his Father's lost children. None of us understood what he meant, really; perhaps we just didn't want to.

Because the Passover is such an important holiday for us—bringing our history and heritage to mind—it causes men's passions to be stirred deeply, especially when in large gatherings.

I was afraid of those passions; for I have seen them boil in men's blood on many occasions, resulting in violent upheaval. And with public opinion split so radically over Jesus, over his message, his miracles, and his claim to be the Christ, I feared that something bad was about to happen.

We begged him, out of desperation, to remain in hiding until the excitement died down. After all, the authorities were anticipating his attendance at the feast and we knew that they were looking for an opportunity to seize him. But he seemed insistent on allowing them that opportunity by his determination to be there.

But that was only part of what was troubling me.

Jesus sensed that I was a little jealous of Mary; and resentful, as well, toward Martha and her. After all, it was because they had requested that he bring their brother, Lazarus, back to life that he was now at risk.

Raising Lazarus, after he had lain four days in the tomb, proved to be the ultimate threat to those who reject his claim to be the Son of the Almighty. They were incensed, at first, because his teachings had exposed their hypocrisy for what it was: selfish ambition. Now, his visible power had made a mockery of their self-proclaimed authority; and their self-righteous pride couldn't undo the influence of his deep humility.

So the holy men in high places were conspiring against him. And I knew from experience that holy men are the most dangerous of them all.

Despite the danger, Mary and Martha hosted a dinner in his honor that evening at their house, in Bethany. They were overjoyed about Lazarus's return from the dead, and wanted to honor Jesus for what he had done for their brother.

The atmosphere was one of celebration, though Messiah's countenance was somewhat somber. Only the most perceptive would have noticed. I did; as did Peter and John. Of course, Mary noticed, as well.

I watched as she and Jesus exchanged greetings. Mary's exuberance and joy changed responsively into an intense appraisal of Messiah's eyes as she greeted him. Her intuition stirred, she seemed to sense that there was a deeper reason for his visit.

He had come needing her, his close friend, this time. Even I interpreted it plainly in his look. She sensed something final in his expression; yet he seemed strong and resolved.

Mary disappeared into the back of the house, her jaw set in determination. She quickly returned carrying a flask of very expensive ointment. With tender devotion, she knelt down at Jesus' feet.

Martha shot her sister a disapproving look. Mary was often impetuous, lavishing affection upon their guests with abandon. For the most part, Martha had grown accustomed to her sister's excesses through the years. And Lazarus's presence at the table reminded Martha that their guest did, indeed, deserve this honor.

Tears welled up in my eyes as I watched Mary anoint the feet of Jesus, the same way I had anointed them one day. Her hands caressed them the way my own had. The scene was almost too tender to watch. I was deeply moved as I relived my own expression of gratitude towards Jesus, not long ago, in the same fashion.

Yet, how different, we two Marys, and what contrast, the two experiences of anointing.

Mary's anointing honored him, while mine put him at risk. Her relationship with him sprung from mutual respect; mine was out of desperation. Her reputation was spotless and innocent; mine, was soiled and ugly.

Observing the depth of communion Mary shared with

Jesus, I grew melancholy. She had blessed him. And though I was glad for her joy, I wished that it could have been me in her place.

My feelings in turmoil, I slipped quietly from the room.

I should have known that nothing would escape his attention. Within a few moments, Jesus found me.

Mary, why are you crying?

I turned to see his frame silhouetted in the doorway. My tears, mingling with the light, hid his features from me. But I knew his voice.

As he moved closer, I could see his eyes clearly. They were pools of compassion and my image was swimming in them.

Mary...

He spoke my name so tenderly. At times the sound of it evoked so much joy, I felt I couldn't contain it.

Yes, Lord.

Jesus sat with me and as his voice strummed the silent chords of the night, he explained that this was his farewell to the other Mary. He told me that Abba had provided strength and encouragement for him in the love of his friends — specifically, in Mary's deep devotion. He explained that he would need that strength in the days that lie ahead.

Then, drawing me into his confidence, he told me that he would need me for a special task in Jerusalem. Of course, I was honored that he would ask.

From the other room, we suddenly overheard Judas loudly questioning whether Mary's anointing was an efficient use of resources.

Messiah's brow furrowed. Giving my arm a tender squeeze, he left abruptly in order to defend her.

Though I wished he wouldn't go, I found consolation in knowing that I, too, would have an opportunity to serve him in a special way... but then, I realized that Judas's protest had interrupted our conversation and he didn't tell me what it would be.

Assuring myself that soon enough, he would tell me, I lay back on my cot, drained from the day's events. I drifted off in the comfort of knowing that he cares when I cry.

I slept peacefully through that night.

But, in Jerusalem, a storm was brewing behind thick clouds of conspiracy.

And within days, Jesus was dead...

Three days after his execution — on the morning following the Sabbath — I awake with the cock's crow. Though it is still dark, I get up. I haven't slept; merely dozed on and off in the raw remembrance of those last days.

Images of Jesus' suffering are seared into my memory, and every time I close my eyes, they appear. I try to convince myself that he must have had a reason — otherwise, he wouldn't have allowed it to happen this way. He could have stopped them—I know he could have. I just wish that he had.

It seems there are no tears left to cry. My eyes are as dry as a desert and nearly swollen shut, for my heart has never left the hillside, grieving where I last saw him.

His words still ring in my ears.

My God, my God! Why have you forsaken me?

Did the Almighty really forsake him, after all? Is that why he gave up so easily?

A wealthy man from Arimathea and his friend who sits on the High Council requested permission to take Jesus' body from the cross. Because I didn't know them, I didn't trust their motives, either.

I watched from a distance as they did it. The sight was horrifying, and I can't erase it from my mind's eye. He was limp and ashen—not the vibrant Jesus I had known.

They wrapped him carefully in grave clothes. I watched suspiciously as they hurried to place his body in a tomb of rock carved from the side of a hill, then rolled a huge stone in front of the cave. They didn't have time to bathe him and embalm him properly. They just stashed him in a sepulcher before the arrival of the Sabbath, and then, they stole away.

I suppose they meant well, but it has become clear to me—in this hasty internment—what I must do; what my mission is. This is what Jesus wanted of me.

My Messiah, still smeared with dried blood and crusted with the salt of his sweat, has been lying behind that stone for three days. And I must tend to him now that the Sabbath is over.

Knowing it will be the last time I will ever lay eyes on Jesus, I am ready before dawn. Quickly, with the assistance of two other women, I prepare the embalming spices. We agree that, though Jesus' life was not spared, his dignity must still be preserved. We also agree that we need to find some meaning for our pain. Perhaps this will provide a starting place. So your mother and Salome agree to accompany me to the grave.

Kneeling together, we make an appeal to Abba for protection. There are those seeking to put an end to us even though Messiah is dead. It occurs to me while we pray, that if God didn't move to protect his own Son, why would he bother with us? I chase the thought from my mind, deciding not to bring it up to my companions.

Hoping to avoid any confrontation with the authorities, and intending to keep concealed the whereabouts of the hidden disciples, we set out as the first hint of light sends its pink streaks across the sky.

Like chains around my ankles, grief weighs me down with the memory of Jesus' final hours. It is difficult now to recall the happy times we shared. Those first few days after my deliverance as he led me to understand my worth in his eyes; the gatherings on the mountainside as he moved among the people, touching them with healing and hope; the cheerful walks through small villages where children ran into his arms as he approached; the peaceful strolls and quiet talks beside a tranquil sea; and the many meals we shared, laughing, and talking as he broke and blessed the bread. It all seems distant and dreamlike now. All of it is gone.

I struggle to remain focused on the task before us. We need to go quickly and quietly about our work, and then vanish.

On our way to the burial site, I suddenly remember the stone that the men rolled in front of the tomb. It will still be there. It had seemed a minor detail when they did it, but now it seems a major deterrent to our mission. Frustrated, I keep walking. And while my companions discuss the situation, I weep wearily from fatigue.

When we arrive, to our surprise, we find the tomb gaping open. The rock has been rolled aside, as if anticipating us.

Amazed, and relieved, we stand staring at it for a moment, until an awful suspicion hits us; *he's gone!*

Panic seizes me, and I quickly stoop to look inside.

I gasp!

To my utter amazement, a young man is sitting on the right side of the burial ledge. He is dressed in soldier's gear—but not like any Roman soldier I've seen. His breastplate is shining like polished bronze and his sword looks like a beam of light. His bare arms are lean, but powerful, and his thighs bulge with muscle from beneath a linen battle skirt, disappearing at the knee into tall, laced boots. He has dark, thick locks of hair and olive skin; but he isn't one of us.

Frightened, I withdraw slightly and turn, whispering to my companions that there is a man inside, but it is not Jesus.

He, himself, is gone. Huddled in fear, we argue quietly about what we should do. If we run for the disciples, the soldier might follow and find them. Yet, Jesus' body is missing, and the others need to know.

Suddenly, it occurs to me that the man himself might have moved the stone — and perhaps even Jesus' body. I edge back inside, intending to speak with him. But he speaks first.

There's no need to be afraid. I know who you're looking for.

I stop short, unsure of what to say.

You're looking for Jesus, the one they crucified.

He continues talking.

He was here, but not anymore. He has risen!

I just stand there, my mouth gaping open, blinking rapidly. What on earth does he mean?

He speaks as if he has some kind of authority, as if he knows Messiah intimately. His next words affirm it.

Go tell the disciples that he is going ahead of them to Galilee. They are to meet him there, just as he told them.

He pauses, waiting for me to respond. After a moment, he elaborates further.

Make sure you tell Peter.

How does he know Peter? My thoughts start rushing to conclusions. I am afraid that this might be a trap set by the authorities. They were so determined to destroy Jesus; and now we fear that our own destruction is close behind.

Sensing my hesitation, he attempts to reason with me.

Don't you remember how Jesus told you, while he was still

with you, that he must be delivered into the hands of sinful men, be crucified, and on the third day be raised again?

And as soon as the words fall from his lips, I do!

I remember!

Wadding my skirt into my fists, I run for the disciples as fast as my feet will carry me.

Stumbling into the room where they are hiding, I blurt out my story.

We went to the tomb… The rock was rolled away… A man said… tell Peter… Jesus has risen!

Peter and John outrun me, of course, and when I arrive they are already inside the tomb—and in shock. The tomb is empty, all right. Even the stranger is gone. The other women stand outside, waiting.

Confused and afraid, the two of them emerge silently from the tomb. It's clear that they don't believe my story. I can see it in their eyes. They probably think I'm suffering from hysteria. There is no denying the fact, though, that Jesus is gone. It leaves them feeling helpless—as I do.

Peter seems almost to be teetering on the edge of despair. He had denied even knowing Jesus the night of his arrest, and now he isn't sure where he can go with his burden of guilt.

As I watch them turn to walk away—their shoulders stooped and their faces downcast—I suddenly feel overwhelmed with loss. I collapse onto the ground, sobbing.

Maybe they're right. Maybe I only imagined the man. Maybe my heart is grasping so hard for something to hold on to, that my mind conjured it all up in response.

I can't leave.

I came here to fulfill my mission, but have found his grave empty. Jesus had said that he would need me here. Yet here I am… and he is gone!

I simply can't tear myself from the place where he last lay. Where would I go? I can barely remember what life was like before Jesus. What will I do now, without him? What will any of us do after all that we have witnessed, and all that we have been through?

Waves of anguish wash over me, and I peer again into the tomb.

What?!

The stranger has returned! I draw back, startled. He wasn't there, just minutes before…

Why do you continue looking here? This is the place of the dead.

My companions, sensing my shock, crouch behind me so they can see. I feel their breath hot against my neck. This time, they hear him for themselves.

Come in and see for yourself. He isn't here.

I hesitate just a moment. Then I stagger forward, into the tomb, the other two stumbling in after me.

Sure enough, the strips of burial linen are lying on the rock ledge, abandoned. The headpiece is folded up by itself and separate from the rest.

My heart is racing, my breath is caught in my throat.

Suddenly, a shaft of light! It blinds us for a moment. Shielding our eyes and blinking into its brilliance, we see yet another man. He is sitting at the other end of the ledge, dressed just like the first soldier—obviously from the same battalion.

I have the strangest feeling that they've been here all along, waiting for us, listening to our conversation, but hidden from Peter and John.

Trembling, we crumple to the ground. Though we don't know who they are, we're certain they're not human—angels, perhaps. We barely have the courage to breathe.

The second one repeats what the first had said.

It's true what he told you. Jesus has risen, just as he said he would!

Too terrified to dispute him, and too confused to understand, we simply gawk at him, quivering.

Appearing genuinely confused by our unbelief, he questions us again, looking directly at me.

Why are you crying?

I barely whisper in response.

Someone has taken the Lord away!

Suddenly, I sense that there is someone behind me.

I turn to see a man standing at the entrance to the tomb, silhouetted by the glaring rays of the rising sun. I squint, but his features are hidden from me.

He asks me precisely the same question.

Woman, why are you crying?

What else do these men expect us to do in a graveyard, but cry? We are the ones acting normal, not they. Though aware of what has happened, they seem completely perplexed by our sorrow.

The man continues to probe.

Who are you looking for?

My heart gives a silent reply... *Jesus.*

I had come to believe that he was the answer to everything.

It was Jesus who had given me the desire to live; and with it, a reason to hope. It was he who had cast the demons from my soul, and with them, the darkness, as well.

It was Jesus who had welcomed my anointing when I was unworthy and unwell; and it was he who had redeemed my shattered reputation.

It was Jesus who had comforted the sad, strengthened the weak, healed the sick, fed the hungry, and mended the broken-hearted—even my broken heart.

But now Jesus is dead. And, as the last ember of my feeble faith is struggling to survive, the stranger in the doorway speaks again.

Mary...

That voice!

Blinking in disbelief, I gasp!

Jesus!

He spoke the one word in the one voice that could convince me that it is he. And at the sound of his voice, his resurrection becomes clear!

I run to him, sobbing with relief.

You're alive!

I fall at his feet, holding them to the place. They are his, no doubt, for the wounds are still there, where the nails had pierced him. But the flesh is warm, vibrant, and full of life. I press my face against them, clinging to him—to the reality of his resurrection.

Mary...

Gently wrestling free from my embrace, he helps me to my feet to face him.

Yes, I'm alive. But, I'm going away to prepare a place for you in Abba's house so that I can take you home with me. From now on, I will always be with you. Now you must go back to my brothers... and be my witness. Tell them you have seen me... ALIVE!

And with that, he is gone.

I jump up and run for the disciples, rushing joyfully toward the upper room. Beating on the door and bursting in, I break through the silence of their disbelief with the words I have never since been able to restrain.

I have seen the Lord!

Philip, I had thought, wrongly, that Jesus would need me to embalm him as a last rite of respect.

He needed me, all right; but not to eulogize, in loving words, the memory of a dead Messiah. Rather, it was to announce the resurrection of the living Lord. Death could not hold him.

The third symbol…

…an empty tomb.

Jesus arose!

The grave had surrendered to the power of love—the power of him who triumphed over death. Silencing forever the inconsolable wail of grief, his resurrection gave promise to us that ours will follow!

On that Sunday, before they knew he had risen, two of Messiah's followers were walking to Emmaus, a small city outside of Jerusalem. They were discussing with a stranger how Jesus had come to such a tragic end.

Imagine their astonishment when Messiah revealed that it was actually him to whom they were speaking!

Consider carefully what those two men said.

We had hoped that he was the coming one.

At last, Philip, our hopes have been championed—it is he!

I pray that the power of his resurrection will likewise triumph, for you, over the enemy who still stalks your soul with the threat of death.

I remain your servant,
Mary Magdalene

THE FOURTH LETTER... COMPOSED IN LATE FALL, IN THE YEAR OF OUR LORD, A.D. 35...

MY DEAR PHILIP,

You are probably aware by now that conditions have worsened for your father. Herod Antipas suffered a humiliating defeat recently by Aretas, the king of Sheba. As a result, he has fallen even further in the eyes of the emperor. He is a desperate man these days, clinging to his scepter with an unsteady hand.

This military overthrow has brought with it other consequences, as well. Julius stopped by the synagogue with sad news. I ran to greet him, overjoyed at the sight of him.

Julius! Praise God, you are safe!

It was an embarrassing defeat, Mary. Herod's moral failings find their equal in his failure as a military leader. He is a weak man and his army is a sad reflection of his leadership. My men fought valiantly, but our orders were confusing and the result was chaos. We never should have been in this war.

What do you mean?

Surely you've heard that Herod committed adultery with his brother's wife, Herodias.

Yes, of course. That evil woman who persuaded Herod to behead John the Baptist. But what does that have to do with the battle with Aretas?

Herod's affair with Herodias scandalized and insulted his former wife, the daughter of King Aretas. Being her father, he was seeking to vindicate his daughter's reputation and appease her wrath. However, Aretas's army proved to be a real threat, which naturally caused Herod's superiors to have grave concerns. It appears that they are tired of cleaning up after Herod's indiscretions, and who can blame them?

I was troubled by the somberness of his tone.

What will happen now?

I have been transferred back to Caesarea. Though it will be good to go home, I will miss this place, and all of you.

Tears sprung into my eyes.

Julius, you can't leave us!

I don't have a choice, Mary. The orders have been issued. I've been reassigned to a battalion in Judea, because the emperor has begun to strip Antipas of his power.

You have been so good to us, Julius.

He rested his large hand on my shoulder.

The good news is, I'll be in the district where Philip went missing. I'm determined to find him.

What will happen to Chuza? I haven't heard from him in so long.

At the mention of your father's welfare, Julius frowned.

I don't know yet. But he is no doubt at great risk, Mary. These political games are ruthless. I pray to your God every day on his behalf, and for Philip.

Julius, he is your God, too.

Oh, Mary, if only I had a legitimate claim to him…

What do you mean?

We Romans killed the Christ.

I noticed how his shoulders slumped under the weight of his words.

But if not for our own religious leaders, it wouldn't have happened. Besides, you weren't among those consenting to his death.

No, but I am a Roman, and he was the Son of the Almighty.

I felt the need to correct him.

He is *the Son of the Almighty.*

You're right, he is.

A hint of a smile touched his lips.

Nevertheless, Mary, any father would be justified in avenging the death of his son, even upon a whole nation.

But the Son who died then, is he who lives now! That's what caused a Roman soldier, like you, to cry out the words my own lips should have, the day Jesus was crucified.

Mary, I remember hearing rumors of that incident after the execution, but I've never heard your side of the story. Tell me about that soldier and what really happened that day.

He seated himself upon the remnant of a stone wall, patting the bare rock as an invitation to join him.

I perched beside him, retelling the event with great emotion, just as I will tell you now…

The centurion has been right here with us the entire time... His job is to supervise the soldiers who drove the spikes and raised the crossbeam into place. I am aware of his presence, but it holds no significance for me in light of what is happening.

I have been pacing, crouching, wailing there at Messiah's feet for six hours, watching him slowly die. I am so near to the cross, I can hear the rattle in his chest, and feel his labored sigh.

The smell of sweat mingled with blood has grown stale in my nostrils. My eyes are swollen from crying and I am spent from the labor of unresolved grief, finally surrendering myself to a place in the dirt beneath him. All I can do is wait and weep. Helplessly, hopelessly, wait.

As Messiah finally expels his last breath, I collapse on the ground, releasing a loud wail that has been building inside my chest.

No!

The wind wails with me, howling into the darkened day. I fall forward, face to the ground, pressing my forehead hard against the rocky soil. The pain offers a peculiar comfort, in contrast to the eerie feeling of disbelief I'm experiencing. I can't gather a coherent thought. I am paralyzed with sorrow.

That is when I hear him say it—the centurion, I mean.

I believe this man was the Son of God!

Not all of us hear him. But those of us who do, cannot ignore it. My head snaps up to see who said it.

It should have been me.

Three days pass…

The morning of the resurrection has been a flurry of activity. It seems I have experienced every extreme of emotion: overwhelming grief, shock, anger, fear, and joy, even to the point of ecstasy. I hardly know what to do with myself.

Being the only witness to Messiah's resurrection has caused a curious sensation in me. I find myself reliving the encounter every few moments, reaching for the reassurance that it did, in fact, happen. It would help if the others weren't so skeptical. As it is, they aren't able to share in my excitement.

The angel's reminder concerning Jesus' foretelling of these events has had a sobering impact on everyone. Peter keeps pressing me with questions; he appears anxious and restless. The conflict raging within his own heart frustrates him. I recognize the tension etched on his face because of my own failings in the past.

But one other thing is bothering Peter. I overhear him whispering to John.

Even if Jesus did come back from the grave, he wouldn't do that, would he?

Do what?

Appear first to a woman?

I don't know, he always had such an unconventional way of thinking.

But any Jew, even Jesus, knows that a woman can't serve as a credible witness —especially a woman with a past like Mary's.

Peter, no one but Jesus would have included them as disciples, either.

You're right. He was always doing things that shocked people.

Even those of us who knew him best.

So, what are you saying?

I'm saying… it would be just like him!

Eventually, Peter slips out the door, hoping that another visit to the burial site might clear up his confusion.

A couple of hours pass. And when he returns, I detect a distinct change in his countenance. Recognizing the look on his face, I run to greet him!

Peter, what happened?

I don't even have words to tell you, Mary. I'm overwhelmed!

You saw him, didn't you?

Yes, I did! With my own eyes! He was just as you said.

He really is alive, isn't he Peter?!

Yes, Mary. He most certainly is!

Hearing the excitement, the others join us. Peter turns to them.

I know that a few of you, like me, questioned whether Mary was simply beside herself, claiming she had been with Jesus.

Peter's animation as he shares his experience is very convincing.

But now I know that Mary was telling us the truth, for I, too, have seen the Lord! Don't ask me to explain it but, he has risen from the dead.

Peter's eyes mist over as he describes Messiah's appearance in detail. And though he doesn't disclose all that passed between them, he seems both humbled and emboldened by it. I feel certain that Messiah must have put Peter's heart at ease, just as he had mine so many times before.

Considering that they have not yet been privileged to witness with their own eyes what Peter and I have seen, the remaining disciples are left in a quandary. They question him.

Why would he appear only to the two of you?

Did he say anything about the rest of us?

Sensitive to their feelings of uncertainty, Peter makes a suggestion.

Everyone seems a little on edge, Mary. It could be because we haven't eaten much since the night of Jesus' arrest. Perhaps if we shared a meal together we would feel a little better.

Joanna and I, in agreement, gather our things intending to set out immediately for the marketplace.

Fearing for our safety, Nathanael wants a word with us.

Keep your head coverings securely in place. Otherwise, someone might recognize you from Golgotha. After all, you women were right there in plain sight.

He, too, seems agitated. Perhaps he wishes that he had stayed nearby as Jesus was dying—now that my story about Jesus' resurrection has been validated by Peter.

Because the streets are teeming with people, we find it easy to remain obscure. The news of Jesus' missing body has stirred the crowds with a morbid sense of curiosity. All of the excitement awakened the Roman authorities to the need to post more military men than usual—just to keep things civil.

Having purchased some salted fish, we hurry around the corner of another booth looking for fresh leeks. Making a turn off the main thoroughfare, I bump into a soldier, knocking myself off balance. The centurion reaches for my arm to steady me.

I peer up from under my shawl to thank him, and gasp when I recognize his face.

It's you!

I meant nothing by it. I simply kept you from falling.

I grasp his wrist with my free hand, pulling myself up directly into his face.

I know you.

He yanks away.

What do you mean addressing me, Woman?

I saw you at the crucifixion three days ago.

Annoyed, he gives me a stern look and turns his back to me.

I follow his movement and come face to face with him again.

Begging your pardon, Sir, aren't you the soldier who was standing guard at the crucifixion of the Jewish rabbi?

What does it matter?

He turns away again.

I follow to face him once more.

Please, Sir. If I might ask you something?

He shifts slightly with discomfort, obviously unaccustomed to speaking to Jewish women.

It's about what you said… just after he died.

I never said a word to you, Woman.

His tone is gruff. He recognizes me, I can see it in his eyes, but it is clear that he wants me to go away.

May I just ask you why you said it? I simply must know! I can't get it out of my mind.

The soldier removes his helmet and turns toward me, rubbing the top of his head wearily with his grimy palm. His face appears considerably softer, much more approachable without the imposing headgear.

He lets the hand which grips his helmet drop heavily to his side, and he pauses and looks in the distance for a long moment. Finally, he responds.

I see a lot of things from my position. I've watched hundreds of executions. But that wasn't like anything I've ever witnessed before.

He grasps my elbow and escorts the two of us into the narrow alley between booths to conceal our conversation. It isn't wise to be seen talking to women in public, and especially to us, women loyal to the controversial rabbi!

He squats down to the ground, Joanna and I crouching down with him, bunching our skirts up around our ankles. I notice his crusty toes framed in by the rough-hewn sandals, his thick toenails poking out the ends.

After some contemplation, he begins talking.

From the moment they brought him in, he was different. He wasn't like the rest of them.

He scrapes the ground with his hand, gathering rocks and dirt clods into a pile.

I've seen hundreds of men die. Most guilty men carry a cartload of rubbish around with them in their hearts, and under extreme pressure, like the pressure that this kind of punishment puts on a man, it ends up spewing out all over the rest of us.

He looks over at me to see if I am following him.

I assure you, we've seen it all. They spit on us, curse at us, hit us with their fists, kick us, and usually say things which women would not like to hear.

I nod. I've heard those kinds of words, plenty.

But he wasn't like them. Not a curse, not a spiteful look, nothing. But it's not just what he didn't say that surprised me—it's what he did say.

I frown, confused by those last words.

What do you mean?

He told someone in the crowd to look after his mother.

He pauses, struggling with his emotions for a moment.

What sort of man does that when he can barely breathe, pushing himself up on a spike, gasping for air?

I wince as he recalls the agony that we had witnessed. My stomach suddenly feels knotted up, churning with fresh grief over what Messiah suffered.

I never saw a hardened criminal care enough about his mother to be sure somebody was looking after her.

He pauses to look at me again, searching for an explanation.

He was the eldest son, and his father is dead. He wanted her in the care of someone he could trust.

I figured as much. I saw the way he looked at her. It disturbed him greatly that she saw him that way.

But she knew he was innocent.

The centurion scratches his chin with the metal prongs on his leather wristband; it makes a crude scraping sound.

Still, it must have hurt seeing him suffer that way, such a quiet man and all. I saw her crying—the way, I suppose, only a mother cries.

He blinks hard against the moisture stinging his eyes. He swears softly.

The thing I can't get out of my mind is what he said when the men were driving the iron into his flesh.

He pauses again and rubs his eyes with a filthy hand. I sense he is stalling.

What was it?

He clears his throat, as if checking his emotions. He

looks away, avoiding my eyes, as he repeats Messiah's words.

He said, Father, forgive them; they don't know what they're doing.

The soldier's voice cracks, and he struggles to suppress the ache inside. I lower my eyes out of reverence for the tears he is no longer able to restrain. This man has witnessed — and probably participated in — more grueling sights than these. His heart has been thickly callused to keep any tender nerve of compassion well covered. But his encounter with Jesus has ripped the callous of hardened skin right off of his heart, and has left all his feelings vulnerable and exposed.

I wait respectfully in the silence for him to regain his composure.

When a man faces death the way he did, worried more about the welfare of the traitors who put him through it than he is about himself, then he's got to be more of a man than anyone I've ever known. It's just not human to do something like that.

Is that why you said what you did? Is that why you called him the Son of God?

Standing up suddenly, the centurion kicks the rocks he had piled up as we spoke. We stand with him, looking expectantly into his face. He seems suddenly drained, his voice still faltering. He is a little frustrated with my probing.

You were right there; did you somehow miss the last words he spoke?

No, I hadn't missed them. They are forever impressed

into my memory. I repeated them slowly and reverently.

Abba, it is finished. Into your hands I entrust my spirit.

A pause lapses between us as the centurion stands looking into my eyes with a curious expectation —as if he is waiting for me to finish —to interpret those final words.

At last, he speaks again with resignation.

Doesn't that sound to you like ...Papa, I'm coming home.

After the resurrection, Philip, Jesus came and went among his followers for forty days. We never knew when he might appear.

At first, he walked through walls to find us crouched behind locked doors, hiding for fear of our lives. Sometimes he would appear at the table and eat with us. At other times, we would find him standing on the periphery of the group, just listening in; eventually offering his perspective, or laughing with us over something someone had said.

It was so amazing, having him back...

His presence is just as it was before he died. He looks like Messiah, only now without the knitted brow —that intense resolve which accompanies a dire mission. His countenance is joyful and attentive.

One noticeable difference is that he doesn't walk among

the crowds anymore—teaching them and touching them. He means for us to take up that mantle. He spends his time with us, explaining things about the kingdom that we don't understand.

The first glimpse of understanding came on his resurrection day…

Hiding in the upper room with the doors bolted, our friends are relieved that Joanna and I have returned safely with something to eat.

Peter and I can't quit talking about our experience with Jesus, along with two others who have come to report a similar encounter on their way to a small village nearby.

Everyone is enrapt in the discussion when…

Jesus appears in our midst!

Do you have anything to eat?

Startled, we stand gawking at him. And though I had seen him earlier in the day, I am no more prepared for this unannounced appearance than anyone else in the room. I respond in a near whisper.

We have some fish and some leeks, here, Lord.

Observing the shock on our faces, he moves to put us at ease.

Don't be afraid! It is I.

He holds out his hands so we can see his wounds.

See?

John takes a step toward him.

Is it really you, Lord?

He opens his cloak so he can see where the spear

pierced his body. Gazing at an open wound in the side of Messiah, John gasps.

How can it be?

Jesus' mother runs to embrace him.

Jesus!

Now John... and Andrew... and all of us at once — running into his arms, sobbing with relief, just as I had done at the tomb. The sight of him is overwhelming, and we simply can't contain our joy.

His arms wrap around us, as many as he can reach, and we huddle there for several minutes, tears streaming, sentiments pouring from our lips. He is smiling and hugging us hard into his chest.

Be at peace, my friends. All is well.

James is the first to blurt out the confession.

Lord, we thought you were gone for good! We thought all was lost.

Andrew chimes in, adding to the admission.

We feared that we would be the next to die.

He nods with understanding, as his eyes search our own.

I know, I know. But you must have courage, my friends, because just as my Father sent me, I am sending you.

There is a long pause. No words, just the meeting of moist eyes as we glance around the circle, questioning each other with lingering looks, uncertain what he means by this.

Jesus shifts, letting go his hold on either side, and moves into the center of our circle. We close tightly around him, our arms locking onto each other's. He rotates slowly within the huddle, reaching to touch each face, looking deliberately into each one's eyes. So close, we feel his breath.

In just a few days, my Spirit will infuse you with the courage, the words, and the power with which you will tell others about my grace—extending forgiveness to all who will receive it.

John gives voice to what everyone is thinking.

But, Lord, only God can forgive sinners.

Up until now, only my Father and I had the Spirit of discernment and of power. But you are soon to be anointed with this Spirit, just as I was. You will accomplish this mission with the same power that raised me from the dead. This is the mission for which I have chosen you.

His silence fills the room. He waits for us to fully absorb his words. Then he nods at us, smiles, and stoops to recline at the table.

Let's eat.

Eight days pass. Still behind locked doors, we have gathered to discuss the events of the past week—a week like no other. Questions have come up about what our immediate future may hold. Peter's intimacy with Jesus during the last three years has provided for a natural transition as he assumes leadership among the group.

We know that Messiah has a plan for us, but because we don't know yet exactly what it is, I think we should stay right here. We know now, with more certainty than ever, that the Lord won't leave us in the dark.

Thomas, who was absent when Jesus first appeared, is very skeptical. Feeling a little on the outside, he becomes agitated and expresses his uncertainty about the validity of our story. It seems his most pressing concern is that we are in imminent danger.

I'm sorry, but I don't agree. We are at great risk here. I say we head back to Galilee.

Peter shows an unusual amount of patience with him, considering that he had missed the excitement of Jesus' resurrection day when he first appeared to speak with us.

Thomas, I agree that there are those looking to put an end to the rumors of a resurrection, and possibly to us, as well, but now that our Messiah has come back from the dead, how can we doubt his power to see us safely through this danger?

Rubbing his beard pensively, Thomas shakes his head.

I'm not so sure, Peter. I don't mean any disrespect but, unless I lay eyes on Messiah myself, I have to question whether you actually saw what you thought you saw. Why, it simply defies all rational thought! And, you have to admit, Peter, you were completely out of your mind with grief… especially after what happened. You know what I mean.

What are you saying? You doubt what I've said? Do you doubt his resurrection?

Unless I touch the nail wounds with my own fingers and place my hand in his side, I simply cannot go along with this. I'm leaving Jerusalem tomorrow morning, first thing.

The words no sooner part Thomas's lips when Jesus appears, standing next to Nathanael. For a moment, we are disoriented, not certain what has happened. But then we realize that it's Jesus—he's standing right here with us. He speaks as if he has been listening in the whole time.

Don't worry, it's just me.

Taking a step further into the room, his eyes looking directly into Thomas's eyes, he holds his hands out toward him, palms up. His voice is gentle, full of understanding.

Thomas, put your fingers where the nails were, and your hand where the spear went through just as you said.

Thomas's eyes widen, his eyebrows arch high onto his forehead. He staggers backwards a couple of steps, speechless. Jesus continues moving toward him, encouraging him with his words.

Don't hold back, Thomas. I'm here for you. Believe everything that you've been told. Believe in me!

Thomas reaches a trembling hand toward Jesus, touching the wound where the nail pierced his hand. Then he falls into Jesus' arms.

My Lord and my God!

Messiah smiles at the rest of us over Thomas's shoulder. Then, placing his hands on his shoulders, holding him directly in front of him, Jesus continues with his counsel.

Thomas, you know now that you can trust your brothers. But you also know what it is to doubt the testimony of an eye-witness. You must help those who, like you, struggle to believe because they haven't seen, then their hearts will be full of rejoicing just like yours is now.

In awe of Messiah's tender heart, I recall to mind how many times I've watched him reassure some troubled soul — often my own.

It gives me peace, knowing that, though everything is different, nothing has changed. He is still with us and forever will be. He lives!

Another month passes. Jesus comes and goes among us causing great joy and excitement. We never know when he might appear. The reality of his dying and coming back to life begins to sink in and we have a sense of anticipation about what lies ahead.

What had appeared to be the end, was, in fact, a new beginning. We are aware of a deeper purpose for our own lives in light of his mission. And we feel that the best is yet to come.

One evening, while eating supper, Jesus comes to us just like before.

My Father will soon fulfill his promise to you.

We sense in his words that something significant is about to happen.

I want you to wait here, in Jerusalem.

He reminds us of what he told us the night he was betrayed.

I am going away, but I will not leave you alone — my Spirit will be with you. It is best that I go away; because when the Spirit comes,

*you will understand everything, and be empowered to take up the
mission where I have left off.*

When he finishes speaking, he asks us to follow him
outside. He leads us out to the Mount of Olives just as he
had the night before he died. We have avoided going there
because our memories of that place are painful, and we still
feel embittered over Judas's betrayal of Jesus.

He tells us how much he loves this old garden, how he
enjoys coming here. Intending to heal our memories of it, he
raises his hands to bless us. I see once more where the spikes
ripped through his flesh. My heart overflows with gratitude
for his willingness to take the nails, for I deserved them—not
he.

*There is forgiveness for all who turn to me for healing. You are
witnesses of these things; for you, yourselves, have been healed. You will
tell people everywhere this good news.*

I watch as his eyes consume us—love lighting up his
face. Then, just as he finishes, just as we think he is going
to lead us back to the upper room, his feet slowly leave the
ground.

At first, I think I'm imagining things.

I blink and rub my eyes. But I'm not seeing things. He is
ascending right in front of our eyes! He is lifted up into the
sky… into a cloud… and carried out of our sight while we
stand speechless and amazed.

Suddenly, the two radiant men—the same ones that I
had encountered at the tomb—appear among us. They are
still marveling at our ignorance and unbelief.

↓↑⌒↑↓

Why do you stand looking into the sky?

It's a good question.

Considering that Abba's Son is on his way home, I suppose we're simply wondering what it will be like when he gets there…

↑

The fourth symbol lifts our eyes to the heavens where the Son, having finished his mission, has returned to his Father…

Jesus ascended.

Philip, what that Roman centurion saw at the cross is what I hope you'll see, too. The soldier's heart couldn't contain the wonder of it all. So abandoning all restraints, he simply stated the obvious.

This man was the Son of God!

Having witnessed Messiah's return to the Father's side, I can assure you, the soldier's confession was accurate.

Sincerely, with the love of my Messiah,
Mary Magdalene

THE FIFTH AND FINAL PARCHMENT...
PENNED IN EARLY WINTER OF THE YEAR
A.D. 36...

PHILIP,

My concern for you grows with each day that passes with your silence. You may not know that Herod Antipas has been deposed, and your father is now in exile. Thankfully, Julius is aware of his whereabouts, and can apprise you of where your father settles.

I'm just glad your mother wasn't here to suffer through this. By the mercy of God, she was delivered from this life before you both went missing. Yet, with both of your parents gone, I, alone, am left to complete the task I began months ago—to make certain that you have heard the whole story of Jesus.

Preferring to speak with you face to face, I begin this, my final letter to you, with mixed emotions. By the time I've finished writing it, my mission will be complete. But know this: my prayers for you will never cease... at least, not until our Messiah returns for us.

When Jesus left us this last time, he gave us the impression that he would be coming right back. I catch myself glancing spontaneously into the sky, expecting to see him any minute. You can imagine that we talk frequently amongst ourselves about his return and we speculate about the reasons for his delay. I've learned that time is a different thing to Jesus than it is to us. He never seemed to be affected by the passing of time. He was never anxious about getting somewhere on time and I learned that it was because he accomplishes his purpose despite the passing of time. He's not bound by it. It's like he is outside of it somehow. I can remember the first time I noticed this about him; you'll see what I mean when you read this, Philip. It was incredible to witness what happened!

I'd only been in Jesus' following for a short time. On this particular day, he was returning by boat to Galilee from the other side of the sea. Those of us who traveled with him knew that he was due to arrive any minute, but somehow, so did everyone else in the area.

It was a windy day and people were gathered at the shore, pressing in to get a good look at him. He was in great demand in those days because he had done several healing miracles locally, and everyone was fascinated by his power. There had never been another rabbi like him.

I feel as if I'm right back in that crowd as I remember what it was like.

The crowd is impatient and on edge; I'm reminded of children waiting for their turn at play—pushing and shoving—irritable with each other. Meanwhile, a storm is brewing on the horizon, which means that their opportunities for healing will probably be cut short.

Someone spies him on the deck of one of the fishing boats just making land.

There he is!

Clamoring to get near him as he climbs out of the boat, they become rude and forceful with each other.

One woman, in particular, catches my eye because of the meekness in her manner—a stark contrast to the rest of the crowd. She seems tenuous and uncertain of whether to approach Jesus. Yet it appears, as he steps ashore, that he is heading straight toward her, causing her heart to race with anticipation—I can see it on her face.

As it turns out, this woman has suffered a great deal under the care of many doctors. As a result of an undiagnosed condition, she has been hemorrhaging for twelve years. Having spent a great sum of money, she is still not well. If anything, she's even worse off than before.

She's here, hoping that the Teacher will finally put an end to her anguish.

Just as she musters the courage to speak to him, a man comes shoving through the crowd, pushing her aside, nearly knocking her down.

Let me through! I need to see Jesus!

He falls at Messiah's feet, grabbing him around the ankles and pinning him to the place. Jesus can't move another step in the woman's direction; he is stopped in his tracks. I recognize the man right away. It's Jairus, a respected religious official who leads synagogue in Capernaum. He's heard Jesus speak many times, and has witnessed several healings. Still, I find it surprising that he is publicly soliciting the Teacher's audience because it could cost him. Jairus rubs elbows with the holy men in high places—the very ones who hold Messiah in contempt.

With both his livelihood and his reputation at stake, I imagine the only possible explanation for Jairus's coming is desperation.

Seeing his distress, Jesus kneels down to tend to him.

Jairus's voice is seized with panic as he informs him of his dilemma.

Teacher, my daughter is dying! Please come and lay your hands on her so that she'll live.

Jesus rests his hand on the man's shoulder. I am gripped with emotion as I watch his compassion express itself through his hands. Helping Jairus to his feet, he says just what Jairus wants to hear.

Take me to her, Friend.

There is really no reason to hurry. Jesus knows that he can heal the girl from where he stands. He knows, in fact, that even if she were to die, he has the power to revive her. But Jairus doesn't know that. And because Messiah is so attentive to his heartache and so concerned for his feelings, he reflects back to Jairus the intensity of his concern. They rush away because that is what Jairus needs.

The crowd begins pressing in from every side. People shoving and shouting.

Teacher, what about my son! He's sick, too.

And I have a boil!

Master, I was here first!

Anxiety twists up onto Jairus's face. He grabs Messiah's elbow, muscling his way through the tense mob.

Let us through! My daughter is dying. We can't waste any time.

But the woman whom Jairus had initially pushed aside is dealing with a desperation of her own. Because of the nature of her illness, she's not only suffering physically, she is suffering the emotional pain of being an outcast.

Jewish people view illnesses such as hers as evidence that something is spiritually amiss, Philip, because our religious leaders insist that disease is the direct result of sin. They declared her unfit for society twelve years ago, when she became ill—isolated in her illness from human companionship and compassion.

This woman, like Jairus, has nowhere else to turn. There isn't another rabbi in the country that would tend to her needs. But she had heard that Jesus was different; that he has a heart for the downtrodden and oppressed. So with no money, no other hope, and nowhere else to go, she has come.

But all seems lost to her when just as he is approaching, and just before she can reach him, Jairus shows up to take him away—and all of her hope with him! As he turns to leave she cries out weakly.

Help!

Her voice doesn't carry over the noisy complaint of the throng.

At that moment, as he is whisked away, the wind whips up and blows the Teacher's robes out behind him. On an impulse, the woman lunges forward and grabs the hem of his cloak.

No sooner does she feel the fabric between her fingers than it is yanked away. But something miraculous has happened: she feels in her body that her illness is gone!

She stands there, stunned, letting the crowd swallow her up. It isn't merely that the blood has stopped flowing; she feels healing coursing through her body like the current of a rushing river.

Twelve years of weakness and fatigue seem to be washing right out of her and strength surges up in their place. The woman is visibly awe-struck.

Instantaneously, a myriad of emotions begin playing on her face.

I'm healed!

Her hand flies up to her mouth, as if to stop a confession that is threatening to blurt out involuntarily.

But I've stolen the blessing.

Suddenly, Jesus stops.

He turns, scanning the sea of faces.

Who touched me?

Everyone in close range draws back slightly, feigning innocence. They all look guilty; but no one is quite certain why.

Peter attempts to get matters back in hand.

Master, what do you mean by asking who touched you? People are crowding in on you from every direction, and you want to know who touched you? It might be easier to determine who wasn't touching you.

Someone reached out for me, Peter. I felt power going out of me.

Jairus's face contorts with anxiety.

Rabbi, we can't afford this delay! How could it possibly matter that someone touched you? Please, let's hurry.

I detect terror in his eyes. The man is frantic with fear.

As soon as Jesus turns, the woman knows that she's been caught. And more serious than the crime of stealing, she is guilty of defiling a rabbi by touching him while she is in an unclean condition. Holy men are never to be defiled by illness or death.

I watch with fascination, remembering when Jesus had first detected the evil spirits within me. I recall how he searched my eyes and studied my face. I observe him now, looking intently for the woman who has tapped his power. I'm curious to see why he is making such an issue of it.

Jairus can't help his impatience. Panic is swelling

up inside of him like a fire blazing out of control, and he imagines his little girl worsening by the minute.

Please, Lord, can't it wait?

An alloyed expression of compassion and guilt flood the woman's face as she witnesses Jairus's anguish. She suddenly flings herself forward trembling!

I'm the one!

Jesus sees her.

She runs to him, falling at his feet, confessing.

I felt healing power come into me when I touched the hem of your garment, and I defiled you in the process. Forgive me, Rabbi!

He bends over her and gently raises her up. He speaks to her in a kind voice, but loud enough that everyone can hear.

You, my friend, are Abba's child; and he has healed you because you trusted him for it. You are to be commended for your faith.

I can't help but smile. I recognize what he's doing. It's so like him. He is rescuing her, just as he did me. Her dreadful disease had tainted her reputation for all those years, and if she were to attempt to resume a normal life based on a flimsy story about being healed by the hem of Messiah's garment, no one would believe her. She needs a witness.

Jesus calls her out into the open, forcing her confession, yes, but standing in as a witness on her behalf—all in one amazing moment!

But then there is Jairus...

While Jesus talks to the woman, taking the time to let her know how much she matters to him and assuring her of the love of God, some men barge onto the scene. It is apparent, from their downcast faces, that they have come bearing bad news.

Jairus senses it, too. He panics, grabbing one of the men by the shoulders, and shakes him as if to release the information.

It's your daughter, Sir. She's dead.

Jairus lets out a wail, and staggers backwards. Tears, coursing down his cheeks.

The man reaches for Jairus's arm, to steady him.

There's no need to bother the Teacher any further. Come with us, and we'll take you home.

Jairus shakes his head violently in response, moaning loudly.

My baby is dead!

I observe the look on Jesus' face as he watches their despair. He turns toward Jairus and grabs him by the arm, speaking with conviction.

Do not be afraid.

Jairus lashes out in anguish.

Why did you delay?

Resolutely, but with compassion, Jesus leads him down the road. Weeping uncontrollably, the grieving man stumbles ahead blindly. The disciples, and some of us women, follow.

When we arrive at the house, Jesus commands all of the professional mourners to leave the room. Only a few of us follow him in.

Messiah stops just over the threshold. He sees the lifeless little girl lying in the center of the room—his countenance visibly affected by the sight of her.

Walking to the cot, he stands over the little girl, studying her. She looks so delicate lying there. He lifts her tiny hand into his own. Smiling, he rubs her skin. He examines her small fingers and, turning her hand over, he observes the palm of her hand, as if in appreciation of his Father's skillful handiwork. He leans over her and brushes a strand of hair away from her face, tracing the contour of her cheek with his finger.

And when he has finished admiring her innocent face, he speaks to her in a soft whisper, as if he is waking her from sleep.

Little one, it's time to get up.

And she does!

So you see, Jesus was able to affect each situation precisely the way the Father wanted him to, accomplishing his purpose in every case. He was thoroughly attentive to each individual, never distracted from his mission, never compromising the welfare of any person present. His response was authentic, compassionate, unhurried and effective.

However, all of that being true, it wasn't obvious to the sick woman at first, nor to Jairus in the moment of delay.

They realized it only as the ordeal played itself completely out.

My point, Philip, is that Jesus is just as attentive and effective now as he was on that occasion. He told us that he would return for us, and we wait anxiously for his coming. But his concern isn't only for those of us who wait. It is for those who don't yet know to entrust themselves to him that he delays his coming. He takes us all into careful consideration.

My prayer is that you will be among those who come to know him before he returns.

And the wait has not been a waste of time, for it has afforded us a tremendous blessing — one which we couldn't have anticipated. Though Messiah told us that he would send his Spirit to us, we weren't sure what he meant by it. But we were to find out not long after his return to the Father's side.

Early, on the morning of Pentecost, only a few days after Jesus' ascension, several of us were gathered in a large room just off the temple porch. We were waiting for the trumpet blast which would announce that we could go inside and worship. It was another Jewish festival — this one commemorating the anniversary of the day upon which God gave Moses the tablets of the Law. That event, though thrilling, terrified the ancients. God descended in fire and

wind and smoke, his voice shaking the mountain upon which
Moses stood waiting.

But, Philip, we were waiting for more than a trumpet.
We were also waiting on the gift that Abba was to send us,
just as Jesus promised. It turned out to be something far
greater than we could have imagined, even greater than
Moses' tablets.

Stay with me, as I tell you of the events of that
unforgettable day...

Expecting the sound of the trumpet at any minute, a
couple of the disciples are having a discussion in quiet tones.
I can hear what they are saying.

*I think Messiah will establish his throne here in Jerusalem.
That's why he wants us to wait here.*

*You may be right, but why would he do that when most of us are
from Galilee? He may intend to uproot the whole system and start
fresh in Capernaum. After all, its location is central to domestic and
foreign commerce.*

Whatever the case, I feel certain it will be any day now...

Suddenly, instead of a trumpet, we hear the sound of
a mighty wind. It rushes into the room, filling the space
and swirling around us, startling and exciting us all in one
instant! We women grasp at our head coverings, while the
men hurry to the doorway, peering up at the sky.

Staring in amazement, we then see what appears to

be flaming tongues settling upon everyone in the room. It is only a minute before it dawns on Peter that this is what Jesus had told us to wait for. He shouts above the roar of the wind.

This is it!

We all turn to look at him. The expression on his face is one of exhilaration.

Don't you see? It's the Spirit of the Almighty! It has come, just as Messiah said it would!

Pouring from heaven with great force upon those of us who are waiting to receive it, the Spirit rushes in — bathing us in power, filling us with bold expression, and equipping us with the ability to do the things we had seen Messiah do while on the earth.

Unlike anything we have experienced before, we are overcome by a compelling urge to boldly talk about Jesus to those who are at the temple. Many of them had been in the crowd shouting "Crucify him!" just weeks ago. We shock even ourselves by testifying so courageously about the grace of God to them — the very enemies of God, for we are no longer concerned over our own safety.

Some of us even begin speaking in other languages — languages we've never learned! I, myself, am empowered with an eloquence of speech I have never known before — much more eloquent than that of a small town prostitute.

Needless to say, the whole episode causes a notable disruption among the people who have assembled at the temple for worship. At first, they think we are drunk. The

effect of the Spirit's power makes it appear that way—an
ecstatic joy which consumes one's entire being. But soon
they begin hearing the message of Jesus spoken in their own
languages—people from every province. Yet it doesn't make
sense to them since we are simply uneducated Galileans.

Peter, suddenly seized by the Spirit's passion, begins to
explain—in words unlike those of a common fisherman—the
reason Jesus came, the reason he died like a criminal, and
how the Almighty has now vindicated his Son's true identity
by resurrecting him from the dead. He shouts at the top of
his lungs.

*Let everyone in Israel know for certain that God has made this
Jesus, whom you crucified, to be both Lord and Messiah!*

The message is so powerful, so penetrating—just
like Messiah's had been—that the people interrupt him,
convicted in their hearts to cry out in repentance!

What shall we do?

Even those who weren't directly involved repent of their
indifference. We are amazed to see several thousand take
hold of the forgiveness Jesus told us to offer them.

It was an amazing day—a day of great revival in Israel!

And that is only the beginning of the amazing journey
upon which we set out—all of us who received the Spirit
that day.

Along the way, we have discovered that we are not only
able to testify boldly about Messiah's redemptive love, but
we are able also to break down the strongholds of Satan:
healing sick people, rescuing those who are enslaved to sin,

and even casting out demons.

We've become well-acquainted with the divine impulse that helps us to discern those whose hearts are dull and insensitive to the voice of the Almighty. We experience revelations of divine power—those which free others held captive to the enemy. And we are intimately familiar with the divine love that moves upon the hearts of men and women, causing them to run into Abba's embrace.

The years have passed quickly, Philip, and our witness has spread throughout the world. The Jewish people have come to believe in Messiah in vast numbers. But that, as you know, has caused a violent rift in our nation, leading the Roman government to turn against our movement.

The persecution has intensified with the growth of our number. Ironically, this has caused the message to spread even more; and our hope shines brighter with every day that passes, as we wait with an eager anticipation for his return.

And at last, the Spirit led us to reach out, not only to the Jewish people, but to all people of every nation. We thrill at nothing so much as the mission that he left us to continue in his absence... until he returns.

As I mentioned, I have mixed emotions, for I, myself, am nearing the end of my journey, Philip. And though I hesitate to bring this final correspondence to a close, I must. My purpose in writing to you is nearly accomplished.

But before I finish, I have one more thing to tell you.

A few days ago, Julius came to see me once more. I can't tell you how relieved I was to see him.

What a sight you are! Welcome back!

Mary, I couldn't wait to see you!

He reached for his pouch which he had strapped over his shoulder and across his chest. Fishing inside it, he smiled broadly and pulled out a beaded leather braid.

My pendant! Where did you find it?

I retrieved it from a soldier in Jerusalem. A cocky young man with a knack for picking a fight.

How did you know he had it?

He was trying to auction it off to the battalion. I just happened to be there that day.

Did you buy it back?

No, I just had a little talk with him, man to man.

He winked, grinning slyly.

I hung it around my neck where it belonged. It was good to have it back.

Thanks, Julius.

He pulled something else from his pouch.

I've made a wrist cuff for Philip, too, Mary.

Oh Julius, it's a work of art! Does that mean you've heard from him? I'll send it with the letter I'm writing.

He shook his head, speaking with conviction.

I intend to make that delivery myself. I heard that he was seen in Joppa recently, so I'm going there to see what I can find out.

You are such a faithful friend.

A pause passed between us. He spoke again, but this time his voice was lower.

Mary...

What?

I heard something else, too.

What is it, Julius?

He looked into my eyes.

Rumor has it that you've been ill. Is it true?

I hesitated, and then nodded.

How bad is it?

I returned his look.

I don't think I'll see the spring of the year...

Julius's eyes moistened and he reached to squeeze my shoulder.

What can I do?

Just find Philip and keep him out of harm's way, until...

He interrupted me. His voice a mere whisper.

Mary.

What is it, Julius?

There was another long pause. I anticipated what was coming.

Don't you think you should tell Philip the truth, before...?

Perhaps I should, Julius.

I swallowed hard.

In the case of young women who fall into harlotry, it isn't unusual for newcomers to be kept on reserve for high-ranking dignitaries. As I shared with you previously, Philip, I became one of those.

A young Roman official, working his way up the ranks and married to a woman who couldn't bear children, asked the proprietor of the harlot house to reserve someone for his exclusive use.

Unlike my former husband, he truly loved his wife, and was unwilling to divorce her. So with her consent, they hired me, a young Jewish maiden, to bear a child for them.

It was awkward, at first. I spent the days doing domestic chores and helping in the kitchen. Then at night, I was summoned, though infrequently, by one of the household servants to attend to the young officer until I should conceive of a child.

Though aware that I was barren, I kept it a secret for fear that I would be put out on the streets. After all, I never really wanted to be a prostitute. I simply didn't know where else to turn.

Miraculously, after only a few months, I did conceive!

The intimate relations with the man were immediately terminated, but I remained with them and with child.

There was so much joy between them. But I was afraid...

I didn't say a word of it, but worried secretly that I might have a daughter, that they might refuse her—hoping for a son—and that she, like me, would end up living a tormented life.

The months passed slowly, and at last, I gave birth to a beautiful baby boy! Never before and never again have I laid eyes on anything as precious as he! My heart felt as if it would burst with love. It was a feeling unlike anything I had ever felt.

I continued in the family's employ for a couple of years, nursing the child until, at last, he was old enough to be weaned.

In the interest of our son, we all agreed that I must return to the house of prostitution after his weaning. We couldn't let the child grow up knowing that he was the son of a street woman. Nor could we afford the scandal if others found out.

The separation devastated us all.

That brief period of my life—the time spent cradling my child in my arms—was the only happiness I had ever known.

And though I couldn't keep my son, at least I have experienced the joy of maternal love. I've tried to console my aching heart with the knowledge that he will be raised by devoted parents—a far better life than I could ever give him. But, still, I've suffered an inconsolable grief over the loss.

Throughout the years, the boy's father intentionally walked him through the streets so I could catch a glimpse of him every now then, as he was growing. The man's compassion toward me has never failed.

Philip, that man was Chuza—your father. And that little boy was you. My son.

It pains me deeply to tell you this. I fear that you will be wounded, maybe even horrified, by my words. It is out of respect for your mother, Joanna, and Chuza—and my own love for you, as well—that I have kept this secret all these years.

Now you will understand that when you fell so deathly ill, it was your Hebrew heritage that emboldened Chuza to ask Messiah to heal you. He was confident Jesus wouldn't turn you away.

That same heritage proved to be dangerous, though, as you grew to be a man, because you bore a greater resemblance to me than to your father. That is why Chuza and Joanna sent you away, to hide you and protect you from the vengeful Herod.

And here you are today, in greater danger still. And your father and I fear for your life, the way he and Joanna did years ago. It is best that you know the truth about your heritage so that you don't put yourself in greater danger, resembling, as you do, the people of Messiah's own race.

I confess to you, though, that there is another reason that I've kept this hidden from you. I had desperately hoped to protect you from the shame of having a prostitute for a mother—a shame with which I am intimately familiar. I wanted to shelter you from the horrors of my own existence. I regret that it has become necessary to risk shaming you now.

You must be shocked at my words, and I fear this might cause you considerable grief. You may even be repulsed by me, and despise me forever. But Julius was right, you deserve to know the truth; though knowing can be painful.

I assure you, Chuza and I have done all that we can to ensure that you have always been in the tender care of those who love you and provide for you in every way.

It is my prayer, my beloved son, that you will not think of me as a vile prostitute, for my story didn't end there. Jesus rescued me from a tragic existence and lifted me from there to live a triumphant life!

My saddest memories were turned into my greatest source of compassion—as I have been privileged to minister to many other women who felt, as I did, so helpless, so lost.

My deepest shame has become, instead, the wellspring of my heartfelt gratitude for the love of God. He took away my tainted reputation and replaced it with something new— he created within me a woman whom others could respect. And though I still find it hard to believe, I was the one to whom the resurrected Messiah first appeared!

I am a sinner, yes, but one whom Messiah rescued, one whom Jesus loved.

That is the woman I hope you'll remember… and all because of Jesus: His coming, his death, his resurrection, his ascension and his promise to return.

The fifth and final symbol represents that for which I wait in hopeful expectation…

Jesus is coming back.

It is the end of the story that is yet to be written upon the timeline of history—the ultimate triumph.

But while he delays, I am busy tending to those who grasp at the hem of Messiah's garment.

I am torn with emotion because, though I had fervently hoped to see you again, I doubt that I will live long enough.

I feel the Spirit's presence—his warm breath brushes gently across my cheek—and it gives me courage to know that, already, Jesus anticipates my crossing the threshold from here to him. My heart reaches for his steady embrace as I contemplate this final journey. My deepest desire is that I will see you again on that day when Messiah returns to take his beloved followers home.

So as my last testimony, I've told you the story through the symbols that I wear over my heart. This is the story of hope that lives within me—the song in my soul.

Philip, Jesus is coming for all those upon whose hearts

he finds engraved the witness of his great love. And though I hope that his coming will be soon, I plead with Abba to delay just a little longer; until you, my son, are safe in Messiah's embrace.

Once the final stroke of the pen is put to the page, the Author will lay down his quill, the Book of Life will be closed, his mission will be complete, and your fate will be sealed.

With all that remains in me, I pray your name will be written there.

Waiting expectantly,
Your devoted mother, Mary

EPILOGUE

A SMALL PAPYRUS REMNANT FELL FROM INSIDE
THE LAST SCROLL AS IT WAS BEING EXTRACTED FROM
THE CLAY VESSEL INSIDE THE ANCIENT TOMB. IT WAS
NOTICEABLY DIFFERENT FROM THE FIVE LARGER
DOCUMENTS. IN A HEAVIER HANDWRITING, THE SHORT
NOTE READ:

To the one whose devotion never wavered,

*Your last correspondence reached me just in time. I hurried to
return to you your most precious possession — your written testimony
concerning Jesus, the Messiah. I am certain it is not safe in my
keeping, for even as I pause outside your grave to write this note, the
persecution worsens.*

*Having fulfilled its mission to me — its truth inscribed as it is
now upon my heart — it will remain in your keeping until the day
when Jesus returns to resurrect you from this tomb.*

*Because of your faithful witness, I will be joining you in the
resurrection, just as you prayed; and perhaps sooner than either of us
had thought. I anticipate that reunion with rejoicing. Until then, I
take up the mission where you left off…*

With Messiah in my heart,
Your son, your brother, Philip

...HE CAME

"Today in the town of David a Savior has been born to you; he is Christ the Lord." (Luke 2:11)

...HE DIED

"And when they had mocked him, they took off the purple robe and put his own clothes on him. Then they led him out to crucify him." (Mark 15:20)

...HE AROSE

"You are looking for Jesus the Nazarene, who was crucified. He has risen! He is not here. See the place where they laid him." (Mark 16:6)

...HE ASCENDED

"And after he had said these things, he was lifted up while they were looking on, and a cloud received him out of their sight." (Acts 1:9)

...HE'S COMING BACK

"'Men of Galilee,' they said, 'why do you stand here looking into the sky? This same Jesus, who has been taken from you into heaven, will come back in the same way you have seen him go into heaven.'" (Acts 1:11)

ACKNOWLEDGEMENTS

One of us did not intend to write this book. The other would not relent. The end result—the book you now hold in your hands—has been an inexpressible blessing to us both. It has bonded our hearts for eternity simply because we spent innumerable hours immersed in deep discussion about Jesus, and shared unbelievable experiences while praying together in the Spirit. Had the book never come to fruition, we would forever cherish the journey upon which it took us. Yet there is more…

To Stan Webb, devoted husband, amazing father, and diligent servant of God. No writer has ever known greater support or encouragement than you have given.

To Mac Owen, devoted husband, amazing father, and diligent servant of God. No one has made more effective use of this method of sharing Jesus than have you.

To Kari Anne, Heath, Cameron, Cherry, Casey, Kyle, and Callie, our precious children, our most honest critics, and our greatest fans.

To Peter Sullivan, publisher and partner, who believed enough in the project to bring it to completion.

To Greg Johnson, editor, literary agent, and faithful friend, who braved the rugged terrain of the (dreadful) first draft; leveling hills, filling valleys, and straightening crooked paths; supporting the authors with untiring enthusiasm and many expressions of encouragement in the precise moments at which they were needed.

To Noelle Roso, editor, literary genius, and friend, who moved a mountain of obligations in her own life to tend to the molehills over which we fretted; who told the truth when it would have been easier to hedge a little; and who saw the work through a critical passage.

To Laurie Bailey, scholar, teacher, writer/editor, and precious friend in the Spirit, whose brilliance brought our work to its finest and final point of presentation.

To Tim Payne, whose noble heart reflects the honest faith of our imaginary Philip. Every writer bears in mind the face of his or her reader, aiming every stroke of the pen at the pupil of that discerning eye. It was your face on our Philip, Tim.

To Mike Keil, Janet Harris, and Beverly Wallbrech of The Resource Agency, marketing and design experts, to whose brilliance we attribute our book title and design.

To Bill Smith, creator of the original format of the symbols.

To Keith Powell, a dedicated craftsman, whose diligent art has promoted the story of Jesus for decades.

To Jean Howard, loving mother and gracious hostess, who cooked and served us many lunches while we worked on the manuscript.

To Ray and Juanita Dickson, devoted parents, wise counselors, and primary encouragers since the beginning.

And to our readers, fellow Witnesses to the grace of God, we extend to you our deepest thanks, as well as an authentic partnership in the Mission set before us all.

*"To him who sits on the throne and to the Lamb
be praise and honor and glory and power,
for ever and ever! Amen."*